of
kindred
and
stardust

Content Notes, Warnings, and Disclaimers

Of Kindred and Stardust contains some explicit content, all of which is meant for adult readers.

This story includes mentions of transphobia and bigotry in a character's past, as well as a subtle reference to that character's deadname. The story also contains references to depression and the loss of a sibling.

Please note the story does employ the use of the gender-neutral pronouns *xe* and *xir*, as well as other such pronouns. These are not mistakes: they are the chosen pronouns of the characters.

To the Pagan community: This one's for you. Thank you to everyone who's been part of the journey, embracing this household with such joy and kindness we will never forget. Blessed be!

To our beloved grove family, Daoine dhen Tamais, and the members of what once was Jubilation, plus others along the way: Knowing you all has been an incredible blessing, both profound and gracious. Thank you for being such wonderful folk and for the safe space, the love, and the light these last 12 years. You're amazing and beyond. Blessings be upon you always. <3 xoxoxo <3

And most certainly to Silbhester, aka. Mr. Fuzzy Paws, Kitten, Your Royal Fuzziness: You might be gone but you aren't forgotten, little boy. You're on every single page of this, having supervised every moment. Love you and miss you. <3 <3 <3

# of kindred and stardust

ARCHER KAY LEAH

CHAPTER ONE
Homecoming, Now in Awkward Party Flavour

Dath Bellin
Sunday, January 4th, 2099, Earth calendar

If ever there was a time to strip and run through the space station naked, today would've been it.

Gods, the thought of it loosened more than one of the stubborn knots in my shoulders. Liberty just by shucking my pants and then some... Not really the homecoming I'd been expecting, but the looks of sheer horror could hold me over for a while if I tried it. At least until I got back from Earth. After that, everyday boring Dath Bellin would return to business, all plants and data, pretending like he didn't make a run for public indecency. But once—just once—*this* Dath Bellin wanted to be reckless, throw care to the wind, and scream, "I'm home, baby!" in all the ways no one saw coming.

Fuck, it'd been a long four years.

Snickering at the lapse in thought, I continued down the long, well-lit corridor, fingertips tracing the bright white and gunmetal-grey wall. Staff bustled past me in both directions, some of them engrossed in conversation, their snug black uniform jackets with the robin's-egg blue and white crossroad patches of ECHO-Crosspoint Space Station welcoming me home. Others rushed towards the lifts with tablets and mugs in hand, likely on their way to the cafeteria down on deck four for a quick lunch before returning to their offices. Most of them ignored my star-struck daze, the occasional brow quirked at how I caressed the lukewarm metal wall, loving the soft pulse and hum of electric wires beneath the surface. I was one shiny control panel away from trying to jack myself into the systems to get at everything I'd missed.

Never thought I'd be so sick of living on my own damn ship, but hey, the day was here.

Not even the day. The year. A whole fourth year.

Why did I agree to this mission to begin with?

I'd been asking myself the same question since the day I left, the answer as lost to me as the parts of my ship, the *Sleipnir*, that got ripped off during our intra-galactic exploration. *Plants*, I've kept telling myself. I went for the plants and stayed for the tourism. The last four years had put my training to the test, stretching my astrobiology PhD to its fullest with more of the universe than my memory could ever hang onto. I'd always wanted to work among the stars, and the mission to the Alpha Centauri solar system had launched entire new worlds at me, forcing me to rethink every classification I thought I knew and reconsider the meaning of life—if it really *was* forty-two, because the hell if I knew anything more than how small I was in the grand scheme of things. I fell in love out there, even with the planets we barely made it off of and the pre-flight check prayers that ended in, "Shit, shit, shit! *Not another bloody fucking incident report.*"

But as much as the mission made all my nerdy botanist dreams come true in galactic brilliance and failed alien bug spray, being back at Crosspoint warmed my heart with the fuzziest damn bunnies. Some of it may have been the pot of coffee I'd practically inhaled in the med bay after arrival. It may have even been being away from the rest of my team, allowing me to think without distractions or wondering if we'd return with the whole five-person crew without befalling a disaster of natural or close-and-way-too-personal proportions. Or maybe it was as simple as considering the station home and wanting to plaster myself to its spaciousness and the fact that it was *stationary… ish*.

In any event, here it was, right where we'd left it in Mars' orbit: thirty decks of space-proofed tin can thanks to ECHO Causroy-Belforte Limited and the relatively new multi-national Milky Way Space Agency. Crosspoint itself was still a baby—only seven Earth years into the project that needed to last for decades longer—but it was worth calling home away from home. Though that was part of the point, to be honest: for more people to call this home. Most of us at the station conducted research, especially on the inter-planetary level, with hopes we'd get a similar station built out by Jupiter. But Crosspoint was more than that: it was a multi-purpose facility, acting as part of an evacuation plan for Earth, a refuge from war, environmental disaster, and any catastrophe thrown at our beloved blue ball, especially if it turned out we could no longer live on Earth's surface in the future. Crosspoint was the lifeboat of lifeboats orbiting in wait.

And one very colourful lifeboat at that.

Damn, what had people *done* at the station on New Year's Eve? Raise a Party God incarnate?

Stopping outside of one staff lounge, I poked my head inside, raising a brow at the trailing red and green streamers still hanging off one of the long steel tables across the room. And glitter, more fucking glitter, stuck on the floor and chairs, content to lay in glistening splendour thanks to the white lights above. I'd been finding the silver and gold specks throughout the corridors, almost as bad as the random clumps of rainbow-coloured cake sprinkles I was certain some space-born Hansel and Gretel had dropped on their way through, drunk as anything.

I didn't know what I'd expected in the wee hours of the morning… night… whatever time we hit the docking bay, but it wasn't all this cheer. Honestly, I'd forgotten what day it was, focused more on getting back, dumping the remains of my gear in my room, and picking up the pieces of my life—whatever was left of it. But roaming the halls, taking in the scents, sounds, and feels… I was ringing in 2099 with the fading echoes of good times and unapologetic joy, clinging to the leftovers that didn't quite want to let go: confetti, empty bottles, and stains on couches I didn't question.

I was just sad I'd missed it all.

Next year, I promised myself, retreating into the hallway. I still had an entire four years to digest mentally, uncertain as to how I truly felt about them. My emotions felt like they'd been stuck on tumble dry for a decade, bashing my thoughts around like rocks stuck in the cycle, dinging off every bit of machine until it looked as battered as my ship.

And life… gods, what was that living thing again? I'd gotten used to new habits, new routines just to survive in a situation we'd made up as we went. I couldn't predict what I'd come back to. I had too much catching up to do; too many apologies to make. Too much sorting of my own life, cataloguing and organizing and slipping through the cracks I'd left, all to grab onto the old reality and pull it close.

I didn't have to figure it all out right *now*, though, and my quiet headache thumped once to make sure I didn't forget it. The sudden reminder killed me as I shoved my hands into the pockets of ratty old blue jeans, my footfalls heavy in my worn brown work boots. I'd been back for eight hours, half of that spent in med bay for the mandatory health checks. In the hour after that, I'd checked in with the rest of my mission crew, all of us unceremoniously dropping our work shit in the RED department's office and running like another one of those damned flesh-eating bugs from P2748-A was after us. Again. And this time, there was no ship hatch to slam before the ugly scale-covered bastard landed and tore a chunk out of someone's leg… again.

It was just as well: five scientists stuffed inside a single ship with more awkward situations than dimples in my ass made us question if RED didn't stand for "Research, Exploration and Development," but something more like, "red as your blood all over my suit if you don't give me space for the next two hours."

Since our parting on sixth deck, I'd spent the last half an hour exploring. Before that, I'd spent two and a half hours in my quarters, reacquainting myself with the rooms that made my quarters on the *Sleipnir* look like a linen closet. A hot shower that actually ran hot had been my first stop, followed by anything indulgent I could sneak in without feeling desperate. I'd never wanted to kiss glass and aluminum so bad.

At least I got this done, I mused, playing with the freshly-trimmed hair at my nape, the strands dark plum as of an hour ago. How dyeing my hair had become a priority the moment I got back, I had no idea, but there it was: short and purple with the slightest curl at the ends. The last time I'd done it was four years ago. The colour had faded out and left me with the ick of natural brown-black for the duration of the mission. It'd looked even worse when it grew long enough to brush my shoulders. Yeah, that had needed to go. I'd roughed it for a while, but I was ready for prim and polished again. Comfort zones—couldn't ever underestimate their powers.

No less than I could underestimate the pull of familiarity, I figured, once more flattening my palm against a wall, the white and grey cold and lifeless next to my olive skin. Something between grief and relief zipped through me—I'd have to acclimate to the station all over again, to all of the things that seemed different since I'd left, or so a part of me believed. That part was still moving through the darkness of space on a ship that felt like an extension of myself, an extra limb of metal and conduits and pumps that'd been battered and bruised but loved in that special way you love yourself on the good days.

It was a matter of perspective; a question of relativity. I'd been assigned to Crosspoint for the last seven years. Three of those years I'd spent walking these halls, with their faint hints of aftershave and hair product mingled with coffee and food. I'd spent countless days cooped up in my office and lab, bounced between them and RED's modest greenhouse, breathing in the calming scent of leaves and fragrant flowers.

Everything was still here, in one piece, and kept in order. The public lounges still begged to be well-loved, the recreation rooms were still heavily in use, and the cafeteria would likely still serve the same things that got shipped here from Earth, mixed with the produce grown in Crosspoint's agricultural houses.

No, the station was the same. I was just removing myself from the picture more than I'd realized.

Or maybe it was the fact that my ship was docked for repairs in the mech bay and it kicked up everything, both the good *and* the bad.

The good: I was hoping—assuming—the mech bay staff could get the *Sleipnir* fixed in time for my trip to Earth in a couple weeks. I'd had four months of vacation promised to me as soon as I'd gotten back, and I intended to enjoy them as soon as possible, after I unloaded some of the work I'd brought back and set up the first batch of analyses. The mechanics assured me they'd try to get the repairs done in time. I just had to remain optimistic.

But the bad, which could've very well crashed into horrible, was that I still felt the gut punch of not seeing Mack there. The bitter sting of disappointment lingered, clamped down on whatever secret hope I'd had that xe'd be in the bay, being every bit the head of xir department and Mechanical Engineer Manager. I could've used a dose of Mack to help me sink into familiarity that much quicker.

Groaning, I pressed a clammy palm to my forehead. Why would Mack be thrilled to see me, anyway? I'd fucked up whatever relationship we had before I left. Went and kicked at the door of possibility, slammed that shit shut, and left Mack with the answer xe wasn't after. Opportunity wasted, and on what? Fear?

Yeah, my social life… Maybe not something I'd wanted to come back to.

"Dammit," I muttered, rubbing at my right eye with the heel of my palm, my headache giving me a solid *thwap*. Tired and off, so very tired and off. My medical exam came back fine, mostly, save for the after-effects of infections I'd suffered in the last six months. It was simple stuff, though; nothing that couldn't be fixed with better living conditions, hearty food, loads of Earl Grey tea—hot, Picard style—and a couple of medications. Most of my current problems shifted among a headache from tension and fatigue, a heaviness brought on by being back on the station, and thoughts of more than one someone I shouldn't have been thinking of but had thought of *way* too much while away.

Le freaking sigh.

Pulling up the thin sleeves of my slate-grey Crosspoint hoodie with its bright Canadian flag patches on both arms, I dragged my feet towards the closest lift and jammed my hand against the touchpad. The fingerprint scan ran its business as usual, its green glow enticing my headache to jab at my left eye socket. A pitchy beep confirmed my existence and set the lift moving, the soft whir of the mechanics only slightly comforting. Damn mechanical engineers. I couldn't even take the lift without thinking of Mack.

Then again, I couldn't stare at a computer without thinking of Kytzia, and that was a *shitload* of computers.

I was so doomed.

Grumbles aplenty, I stepped into the lift and pressed hard on the keypad, praying I could make it to my quarters on twelfth deck without anyone else stepping in. I did *not* need more people, just quiet.

Quiet was granted, the trip quick and lonely, and I found myself rushing through the aft corridor to my room more than sauntering all cool and casual. Thankfully the hallway was peaceful, no one else in sight. Being just after noon, it wasn't a surprise.

My quarters were no different than how I'd left them years ago, save for the stale feeling off that first step or five into the room earlier. All white with bright cerulean-blue curtains around a big bay window, the suite faced the expanse of asteroid belt that separated Jupiter and its friends from the sunny side of the solar system—the very reason why this station was called Crosspoint. Off to my left, the sliding door to my tiny bathroom was partially closed, hiding the soiled towels drying over the shower stall. Just to the right of that, the half-dozen cases of personal items I'd taken on the mission sat beneath the window, their white shells dull, marked, and worn compared to the pristine wall of the station.

The bed to my right was the only thing I cared for at the moment, though, the comfy mattress and clean pale blue sheets making me forget the four years in a bunk. There was nothing wrong with wanting to dive in and hug it, right?

Venturing towards the bed on a lazily-footed arc, I glanced at the nightstand and black desk on the other side of the bed, seeing nothing but rainbow-coloured computer cords and a dusky purple desk lamp. Not far from them, a modest greyish-blue dresser was built into the wall next to a round table and two chairs tucked into the corner by the window. The table needed a light dusting like everything else, though the dresser…

I crossed the room before I realized what I was doing. When I'd been in here earlier, I'd ignored the items on my dresser, but now they had my attention, drawing me in with their own gravitational force: my personal altar, a connection to home and the life beyond it, connecting spirit to universe and offering the calm I needed to balance the chaos of living. I'd missed this space, these items. I took a deep breath and let memory wash over me, soaking in whatever energies lingered.

Closing my eyes and trying to remember the last time I'd stood here, I played with the silver chain around my neck. Three items hung on the chain: a custom-made, silver Druid Awen pendant with two white quartz stones and an amethyst, all set inside a wreath of entwined bronze, silver, and gold metal bands; a silver triskele from my sister, Callie, purchased from one of the Highland Games we'd visited as teens; and a silver Tree of Life adorned with a multitude of tiny amethyst, onyx, moonstone, and sapphire stones, a piece I'd more than gleefully shelled out money for at a Pagan Pride event when I'd been in university. I'd fondled these pieces more times than I could count throughout my life, a habit whenever I was stressed or lost in thought. Gods knew I was both right now, needing something—anything—to calm my nerves. Wasn't a homecoming supposed to give you peace? Shouldn't it have been exciting? Joyful? Welcome like an old friend at your door on a cold night, standing there with vodka in one hand and video games in the other?

So then why did I feel like throwing up and hiding in the dark?

A cleansing, that's what I needed. Cleanse the altar, clear my thoughts. Reconnect with the spirits and pray they'd guide me back to where I was supposed to be.

I scurried through my room, rummaging and gathering everything I needed: fresh candles and incense sticks from the dresser; rose water and cheesecloth from my nightstand. The precious few items I'd taken with me to Alpha Centauri, since I didn't have the space or the safety to take anything else. My altar for the past four years had been only slightly bigger than my work tablet, a barely-there thing in my private quarters on the *Sleipnir*. Having the full thing at my disposal right now was more my everything than I'd ever admit.

Priorities: I had 'em in spades.

Once all of the gathered items were on the bed, I moved everything from the top of the dresser onto the bed, too. After a quick wash of my hands, I cleaned the top of the dresser with the rose water and cheesecloth, my touch light as I hummed along to the random tunes skipping through my mind. Next came the purification: a touch of lighter to the sandalwood incense set the potent scent swirling and wafting through the air, filling the space as I swept the stick over the altar and all the way around it. The fragrance nearly choked me; it'd been too long. More than one cough slipped out, forcing me to place the incense on my nightstand, well enough away.

Cleaning the altar items and placing them where they belonged took the most time. The Goddess candle was first: a tall, wide, white pillar candle that sat on a colourless glass plate in the centre of the altar. In front of it, a trio of shorter white candles stood on a pewter plate decorated with Celtic knots and triskeles: a representation of past, present, and future. With the foundation laid, I placed other candles of various colours around the Goddess candle in a semi-circle, including a black pillar candle for the deaths, losses, and the grief that was, is, and will be.

The final candle was a rainbow-striped candle for the Ancestors, one of my favourites of the bunch. Lighting it always returned me to people I needed to remember—loved ones from my past who were no longer alive and guides from my youth that time had snatched away, leaving their essence to drift from one day to the next on the back on recollection.

More than once on the Alpha Centauri mission, I'd found myself nearly joining those Ancestors. I'd have to sit with that candle for a while and share my perspective with the ghosts it raised. Maybe I'd find another guide lurking in the quiet, past the Veil, willing to share their wisdom and help me make sense of it all. Going face to face with mortality scared me but staring it down in the cold of space piled on a new loneliness I wasn't ready to deal with.

I drew away, leaving that darkness there for now. Dealing with it would require more than time here: a trip to Crosspoint's psychologists was certainly on the books, for however long it took to make peace with what I'd been through.

For now, setting up the rest of the altar would do. My collection of gemstones sat neatly on an oak plate off to the right-hand side, joined by a pinecone, a seagull feather, a piece of shale, and a vial of dirt from Mars: reminders of the Nature Kindred, both on Earth and in space. On the left side of the altar, I set down a silver bowl filled with water from Lake Ontario, along with a box of matches and a plate of incense that carried the scents of lavender, dragon's blood, and cedar. A green statue of a willow tree finished the triad, accompanied by my colourless glass wand with its amethyst crystal at one end and three silver wires coiled around the shaft.

Satisfied with my efforts, I struck a match and lit the Goddess candle first, followed by the other candles, with more than one moment spent on the black and rainbow candles. I twisted off the rings I usually wore and slipped the collection of pentagrams, triple moons, triquetras, and spirals into a brass bowl that would sit on the altar for three days to pick up better energies. We'd all been put through the wringer a few times over. Though my talismans… those would stay around my neck for a while longer. I'd recharge them overnight, while I was asleep, assuming I could stay out of trouble until morning.

With a snort, I sat on my bed, cross-legged with my eyes closed, my hands in my lap. Listening to the muted sounds of the station, I slowed my breaths the best I could, dismissing the slight rattle that haunted my lungs from a cold, and pushed my thoughts onto a track of reflection that retreated from Alpha Centauri, Crosspoint, and everything between here and Earth. I thought of where I'd grown up, some nerdy little kid in a suburb in Toronto, so accustomed to city life but attached to what grew from the earth, organic and raw and amazing. I'd spent more time watching vegetables grow than eating them, refusing to accept I couldn't live in a greenhouse for the rest of my life. I'd despised caterpillars and beetles for more than a year for devouring that which I'd held sacred even as a ten-year-old, choosing to make friends with worms and fungi instead. All the wonder I'd had; all the need to grow up and reach for the sky like the trees, pushing forward towards the sun. How like a leaf I was now, caught in the air and drifting towards a new place to rest. Maybe that's what we all were in the end: individual leaves on the universal tree, dancing, waving, and taking in the light until the universe let us go, giving us its blessing to find our own way and a place to fall, rest, and leave the world with whatever we'd done along the way.

Reaching past my thoughts, I searched for the grounding point I sorely needed, digging around for the hope rooted there. I needed to touch that okay-ness, to taste certainty and meld back into life one breath at a time; to find a gentle place to rest before being swept up again.

Home: that was a tender place, a warm thought. Crosspoint was my home out here, but my heart would always belong to Earth. To whatever house my parents lived in. To my old townhouse in Oshawa I'd leased to Callie and her wife before coming to Crosspoint. If I could see it now… I'd cry and kiss the asphalt, no lie.

I'd have my chance soon, though. So soon

with the way time ticked away, stealing moments before I'd managed to catch them, like dandelion fluff on the breeze. I wanted to spend two weeks here—three weeks, tops—sorting business, then go home by the end of the month. Vacation had never sounded so much like paradise, right down to the cars and malls and kids. Four months Earth-side for some R&R? Yes. Dear gods, *yes*. I had family to pull close, friends to pester, and my Druid grove to catch up with. Home-home, where I could touch the earth, say my thanks, and breathe the fresh air. Slip my feet into the lake and skip stones across the surface—at least try, since I usually chose rocks that sank before any skipping happened. I needed to take in the sights of humanity, the scents of the city, and feel closer to the hum and thrum of life on our over-populated planet that still worshipped celebrity, prayed for the favours of lottery, and lived life through their screens.

Just a couple weeks—I could do that. Then I'd be out of here by the end of January and celebrating Imbolc on the first of February with my grove. It sounded perfect. The holiday was one of my favourites, what with the Wheel of the Year spinning into the light and ushering us towards the spring equinox as the Cailleach moved on. It offered new beginnings, a fresh outlook for the year, and inspired hope for what existed beyond the darkness on its way out behind us. There was the essence of rebirth and renewal, right down to the smallest seedlings fighting for their chance to grow up. All of the best medicine I could use right now—

Save for my stomach, which growled like a beast. Loudly.

Rumbles took over almost immediately, because fuck growling. Rumbling like a grouchy earthquake was all the rage.

Huh, who knew I was starving?

With a sigh, I considered resuming my meditation, only to have the thought kicked to the curb by some sound from my guts that leaned a little too far on the side of alien chatter. Reluctantly, I dragged myself off the bed and took a moment to find my feet. I might not have been able to ground yet, but the rest of my body seemed interested in sticking my face to the floor.

Standing at the altar, I circled my hand over the candles, said my thanks for saving my ass from just about everything that wanted a piece of me, and blew out the flames.

Welcome back.

Turducken. Deck four smelled like turducken.

Good gods, had they saved a slice of Winter Solstice for me, too?

Standing outside of the lift, I stared through the open doors in front of me, stuck on stunned. A kitchen. I missed that. A big cafeteria that could seat at least a couple hundred, if not the whole three hundred or so of us at the station. I missed that, too. And food. The hustle and bustle and… and…

Poutine?

A tall, bald guy I didn't recognize walked past me with a smile on his face and a jaunt to his step, the scent of fries slathered in dark gravy and cheese catching my attention more than anything about him.

I made a beeline for the cafeteria, desperate for the taste of something that wasn't the food packets and rations we'd survived on during the Alpha Centauri mission. *This* was familiarity wrapped inside a pancake blanket of welcome, and I really *could* be bought by way of my stomach.

I snatched a steel tray from a table near the door and observed the expanse of room to my left: wide, open space with metal tables that sat eight and lightweight chairs that could be folded up and stored. The walls were white with red accents, lines of small vinyl flags strung up around the room to honour the nations represented on the station. The cafeteria wasn't full, though a few dozen staff and personnel still lingered on their breaks, the green digits of the clock on the wall pushing 1400. It looked like an entire team was having a work meeting at a table in the back, their things on a second table that overlooked Mars through the floor-to-ceiling windows of the exterior wall.

Not recognizing anyone, I continued towards the counters and buffet tables to my right, flashing the kitchen staff grateful smiles. *Turkey? Poutine? Mystery salad from the agricultural bay? Yes, yes, and yes. Curry and rice? Pile it on, right there on a second plate with the stroganoff… and tea? Please, yes! I'll beg if I have to. Hell, skip the cup— hook me up to an IV, 'cause I'm running on fumes.*

Carefully balancing my full tray with both plates and a jumbo mug of steaming rooibos tea, I shuffled towards the closest empty table, fully intending to sit down and plow through everything with a return for seconds.

Intentions. Funny thing, those. I got smacked with so much intention right then you could've punched me over with a goddamned cotton ball.

Mack and Kytzia.

Mack *and* Kytzia.

At a table, tucked in the back right corner, being all close, kissy-face cuddly…

And not sparing me so much as a look. Did they even know I was in here?

Apparently four years could work a shitload of magic, because those two together had *never once* pinged my "*What if?*" meter. But this, here, now—

I nearly choked as Kytzia kissed Mack, her

fingers stroking xir neck and tangling in Mack's long, dark brown-black hair. Kytzia could kiss so sweetly, caress so lovingly, then turn it all around and jump you like a tiger tackling its prey, where the only words worth saying were, *"Yes, steal my soul."*

Meanwhile, Mack… Mack had always made sure I left xir side in the morning like a responsible adult—only I'd stumble right back a minute later, unwilling to leave completely, and we'd wrestle it out lovingly until I *did* leave to let us start our day. I'd kept going back as if Mack held the keys to everything inside of me.

But standing here killed every bit of me, even more than when I'd broken up with them both four years ago. We were separate entities then: Mack and me, me and Kytzia.

But it had never been Mack and Kytzia. Never all of us.

And now. Now…

I noticed more changes as I stared at them, the details slowly sinking in. The last time I saw Mack, xe'd had shorter hair, long enough to style into spikes. Even then, Mack hadn't been a stranger to hair extensions, chain links, glitter, and anything that complemented xir fantabulous collection of earrings.

It appeared most of that was gone, traded for a shaved head on both sides with a six-inch strip of brown-black tresses that fell to Mack's mid-back. Mack had tied those strands back at xir neck—likely to keep it out of the way while xe worked.

Despite that, I didn't doubt Mack's eyes remained the rich brown I remembered, no contacts to change their colour, and xir skin was the same beautiful light brown with the warmest golden tone, thanks to Mack's Brazilian side of the family. And the piercings. Gods, the piercings. Please tell me Mack still had the nipple hoops…

All of which was for Kytzia to enjoy, I realized with a solid thump in my heart. Kytzia and anyone else Mack was seeing.

I turned my gaze to Kytzia, whose lush, deep red hair was sleekly cut to her shoulders, with bangs she'd flipped back and pinned down so there was a slight bump in the front. Cotton-candy-blue and neon-purple highlights broke up the red, different from how she'd done it before as if a rave had exploded in her hair. Her porcelain-fair skin was still rosy with the cutest damn freckles, and part of me was dying to know what coloured contacts she wore today; certainly not the white films or cat eyes, but would her hazel irises be hidden behind another colour? Just what did Mack see as xe laughed and tickled Kytzia's arm? Did xe love the blue, pink, and purple butterflies tattooed on Kytzia's left ankle like I did? What about that tattoo in the small of her back with a small band of blue and yellow alien creatures with octopus tentacles and floppy ears?

My irresistible mechanical engineer. My brilliant systems analyst... All of it gone, because apparently I was a massive screw-up who couldn't have made a worse fucking decision.

An epic screw-up who'd been staring a little *too* long. Mack finally looked at me, meeting my gaze.

Blushing to high hell, I ran from the cafeteria, hot tea sloshing over the rim of my mug and burning my fingers. Precariously balancing the tea on the tray, I rammed my hand to the scanner and bit my tongue in wait.

I was thirty-five years old, for fuck's sake. I had the courage to live on a station that was still being tested as the first of its kind and manoeuvre a ship through the Kuiper Belt, but I couldn't say a fucking hello to those two.

<hr>

The journey to my quarters was far longer than I needed, the tray shaking in my left hand as I gripped the mug for dear life. I'd had a thing for both Mack and Kytzia for a while: Mack for six and a half years, Kytzia for five. For a brief span of time, I'd hooked up with them both.

Mack and me, we'd kept it simple and chill. After meeting each other at ECHO's ground station in Toronto and going for several coffee dates before learning we'd both been assigned to the space station, we'd pursued a casual, open relationship. That'd been six years ago, and my demisexual, slow-to-burn romantic nature hadn't fazed Mack one bit. It worked great for me, seeing as I hadn't been looking for anything serious, particularly since Crosspoint was my first project in actual space and not a simulation or dream. I was focused on my work, and I'd signed up for the exploration missions, so casual was good. Practical, even. The others Mack dated at the same time hadn't bothered me, either. We had a plan, an agreement, and neither of us complained.

Six months into my relationship with Mack, Kytzia and I struck up a fling, even though I hadn't been seeking another relationship. Kytzia and I had worked together on the RED system, getting our department completely patched into the main network and stopping the frustrating glitches at a time when she'd doubled as a technician. Long days at work extended into after-work drinks weeks later, then soon fumbled themselves into a kiss in the observation lounge and a casual relationship of our own. I hadn't been looking for anything beyond a professional relationship with her, but fuck if I didn't just fall into it. She was always too damn adorable to say no to, so I let her take me along. We'd had it good and no one complained. Mack, me, Kytzia—we'd worked it all out.

But the next thing I knew, everything changed so quickly, too fast for me to make sense of it or even process it beyond stumbling over my questions, especially, *"What do I do?"*

So many hasty decisions were made then, way too many to count.

A month before I left for Alpha Centauri, Mack brought up exclusivity. With me scheduled to be gone for at least three years, xe wanted to know how I wanted to play it—play us—while I was away, then when I got back. Mack would wait, xe'd said, especially since Mack had ended xir other flings several months before. Meaning I was the only one xe was seeing and Mack was ready to try committed, taking our relationship to a new level.

Gods, I'd wanted to. I wanted to go there with Mack and everything we could have. I still did.

But Kytzia... I couldn't just leave her.

Only a few days after Mack's conversation with me, Kytzia said she wanted to go steady with me. She'd put up with my relationship with Mack for a year and a half, and while she'd still be willing to go along with it, she was hoping I'd commit to her instead of being a fling. The whole time we'd been together, she hadn't hooked up with anyone else, just me.

And when she and Mack were in the same space? *Fuck,* it was all kinds of weird. *So much* awkward, of unfathomable proportions.

I was shoved into a burning spotlight in the middle of the chaos between us and expected to make choices—none of which I'd been ready for, or even emotionally capable of working out at the time, not with my first exploration mission right around the corner.

I didn't know what the right answer was. Yeah, I had a thing for Mack. I wanted to know what we could have if we really buckled down and gave it our all, but I felt similarly for Kytzia. *What kind of a choice was I supposed to make?* And what had happened to casual? Just *when* had that fallen through the cracks?

Two weeks. I'd sat on their questions for two weeks, stressing over the smallest things I hadn't already been stressed about.

A week before I left, I turned them both down.

I told them I didn't want anything committed with either of them… even though it killed me.

I lied and buried myself in my own personal hell.

That entire last week before the mission, I hid from them, avoiding as many people as I could while I slogged through the last pre-mission bullshit, pretending like I was okay.

Except I was so far from that then, and I was *still* light years away from *okay*. The mission hadn't been the only thing screwing with my head for the last four years: I'd spent the first year kicking myself for being a shitastic boyfriend, the next two trying to forget, and the last year wondering *what if*. Because I'd had a lot of time alone with my own thoughts, and some of them were ugly, full of regret and punishment. I'd spent days in my bunk, questioning what Mack and Kytzia would be doing while I was in the next solar system over. I'd asked the universe if they were happy, if they hated me, and if coming back home would be all sorts of messed up.

Those feelings I said I didn't have ate me alive, and now I roasted on the open flames of *what the fuck did I do?*

I couldn't choose between them. *That* was the truth of it, the single fact I clung to. I'd worried that if I chose either Mack or Kytzia, I'd still be stuck on the other, regretting the decision to commit to one over the other and always hold a part of myself back, which would be completely unfair to them both. So I told them I didn't want them and pretended to move on, hoping that letting go was better for us all.

Now I saw just how well that had worked out. The ridiculous warm fuzzies in my gut didn't make anything better, the image of them as a couple, being so sickly cute and romantic…

Grunting, I dropped my food tray onto the table in my room and collapsed into a chair. It was too late to tell what we could've had. Way too late for everything. Hell, I'd be all sorts of late for my own fucking funeral if someone weren't in charge of getting me there.

Oh, but wait, I thought, a strangled laugh slipping out. *I'm already late for that funeral where they're concerned. Or maybe I'm just really fucking early.*

Gods, I was too young to be giving these many sighs over life, one right after another in a succession that didn't want to end. Seemed someone had left the *happy* out of my homecoming package.

I wanted a refund.

CHAPTER TWO
Promises, Plans, and Perfect Payback

Mack Ainsley Tsallis

Oh, hellll no, did Dath just walk out of here, no hi, no nothing. Just shot off like something bit his ass—or his junk, from the expression on his face.

"Damn, guess shit really *is* that bad," I muttered, more shocked at seeing Dath than caring about what came out of my mouth. Just… it'd been a long time, practically eons away. I'd known he'd be back soon, but… Christ, it'd been such a long time.

Kytzia jolted away. "What?" she asked, her concerned frown instantly making me feel like an ass. Red brow furrowed, her gaze searching mine from behind purple and green contacts, she dropped her hands to her lap. "What shit? How bad? What don't I know?" The more she questioned, the stronger her Kiwi accent came out.

Ugh, yep, definitely an ass, me. Her accent always thickened when she stressed out, and with the work she was doing on system upgrades to make our IT more efficient despite the interdepartmental headaches that came with the various projects, I really didn't need to add to that stress.

I gave her a sloppy smile in apology. Throwing in a wink for extra measure, I hugged her close and planted a loud smack of a kiss on her forehead, the scent of her floral shampoo filling my nostrils. Lord, I loved the stuff. It was just so her, always sweet and colourful on every single sense I had, never far from where I always wanted to be. Happy. At peace. Content to stay.

All the reasons Dath had pushed us away—an assumption I'd stake my life on, because his, *"I don't want you; I don't want this,"* sounded a hell of a lot more like a load of bullshit in hindsight than anything.

Worse part was that Kytzia and I both knew he'd completely lied, but he'd never given us a chance to realize it and find a new solution before he'd completely shut us out and then left.

Apparently, that door was still firmly slammed in our faces, even if all we wanted was to crack it open and have the simple chance to ask *one* question, plus maybe offer a touch of hope.

"Nothing, *meu docinho*," I said softly, the endearment appearing to give her enough reassurance to let her sink into my arms and hug me back. With Kytzia, I always opted for the Brazilian Portuguese terms of affection first in the tensest moments, and if they failed to comfort her, I still had my basic use of Gaelic ones. Seemed she loved my Irish-Brazilian Canadian-ness as much as I did. As much as Dath had.

Goddammit, Dath! You're still screwing with my head. Hers. Ours. And now… now…

I squeezed Kytzia gently, clinging to her lightness and the soft, stretchy fabric of her dark blue Crosspoint pullover with its Australian and New Zealand patches. Beneath that, she wore charcoal-grey trousers and a lilac shirt, its pale hue so much softer than the black t-shirt and cargos I wore. And the grease. That was grease on the edge of my right hand and wrist, a souvenir from brushing up against someone's ship last night while I tinkered with their gauges and pumps during my off-hours. I hadn't even been to the mech bay today, only to my office on the deck above that; I'd been too busy with meetings, listening to men in suits drone on and on, then zipped headlong into more than one heated dispute with suppliers, raking them over the coals for screwing with specs and orders—all of which had distracted me from realizing that Dath's ship was more than likely parked in the bay.

The rest of today could very well be shot.

"You're not getting out of it that easily,"

Kytzia murmured in my ear. She pulled back, still frowning as she tugged on my ponytail. "Spill."

Crap. She was giving me one of her looks—the *try that again and you'll hear about it for the next two weeks* look. How twisted was it that I wanted to kiss that look a hundred times, just to keep it close and appreciate it for all it was worth?

Honestly, though, how was I supposed to answer her, sitting in the cafeteria and reeling over who'd manifested out of nowhere only to run away again?

With a sigh, I rubbed my forehead and closed my eyes, willing on the bitter truth like ripping off a bandage. "Dath," I relented, almost whispering his name. "He was here."

Kytzia all but jumped back in her seat, sending it squealing backwards towards the window that gave a stunning view of the vivid red surface of Mars. "*Dath?*" She glanced around the cafeteria frantically, her mouth open as she peered at the tables and doorways. "Where? Just now?"

"Few minutes back," I mumbled. "He left, though. But I saw him looking. He was watching us."

"Oh." The quiet word fell between us with so little effort, its dejection as heavy as the disappointment in Kytzia's eyes. All of the reason why I slipped my arm around her shoulders and drew her close again. "How'd he look?" she asked, burying her face in the crook of my neck. "Good? In one piece?"

In one piece, yeah, but I hesitated to say anything that suggested *good*—at least not in all the senses of the question. He still had that olive skin with a peachy glow I'd always loved touching, and those mossy-green eyes that reminded me of home so bad, even when he insisted they were as beautiful as a swamp he'd never be caught dead in. Always a matter of opinion, I'd told him, loving it even more when he remembered to wear his glasses while working, especially when he'd slip them on top of his head and forget about them. The way the silver frames would push back his hair and hold tight the way I wanted to.

And that rich plum colour to his hair, its darkness calling to me, and the soft curls at his nape... A hundred memories hit hard, neural flies on the grey matter screen, enough to crush parts of me I thought I'd dealt with since we broke up.

But *good*? I couldn't say that much. As gorgeous as he was, he'd looked like utter shit, almost like he'd fall over any moment. He looked too thin, too worn, too beaten down and old. Christ, he looked like he'd gained more than a few years on his trip, edging him way too close to my forty-two years despite him being only a year younger than Kytzia.

"Tired," I said, swiping her cheek. "He looked so tired, babe. Here but not here, you know?"

Kytzia sighed as she nodded, playing her fingertips over my left wrist and up my arm, then down all the way to the Iron Ring on my pinkie finger. We'd known this day would come, when he'd saunter back into our lives. But, damn my soul, I hadn't been ready.

From her silence, it seemed like she hadn't been ready, either. Knowing he'd return, and him finally being here, were vastly different things, neither of them easy to swallow. All of the things it meant, including the problem of how we wanted to convey our thoughts to him even though he could turn around and reject us again.

Kytzia and I, we'd talked about it not so long ago, but there'd been no simulation to test-run, no prediction of what we could expect. It was all a matter of organic emotion and praying that four years had changed his mind. Or opened it, at the very least, because I could do open.

As for Kytzia: I knew she'd bash down every door and window until all of them *screamed* open, and I'd give her the sledgehammer to do it.

She was up before I could think of anything worth saying. "Come on," she said, picking up our single food tray with its empty plates and mugs. "You've got time before you head back, yeah?" Slipping past me, she tugged on the back of my t-shirt. "Let's go get some air."

Ah, code for *screw this joint, we're off to get personal with each other.*

I followed her to the main entrance with only a short detour to drop the tray on the receiving racks in the alcove just left of the doorway. While we waited for the lift, I dropped my arm around Kytzia's shoulders again, the foot of difference in our heights more obvious now. We stayed close on the way up to deck fourteen, then leisurely strolled the silent corridor, passing several quarters on the way to Kytzia's.

Despite the three years we'd been together, we still bounced between her quarters and mine on deck eighteen. Most of the time it came down to which room was closest, seeing as we tended to work at opposite ends of the station, moving throughout as our responsibilities dictated. As much as I would've loved to spend all my time in the mech bay, wrenching things together with my team, it really didn't work that way. All the while, Kytzia spent most of her time cooped up in offices, working magic like some fairy godmother of tech. Which was why I didn't doubt that despite all of her stressing, she'd do something clever and make all her work problems *poof* themselves away.

"I think we need to revisit our earlier discussion," Kytzia said, glancing up, her tone dead serious as she broke through my thoughts.

"What? About Starman and the Tesla finally

reaching the end of their journey after eighty-one years?" Because anything that included launching an electric car into space with a mannequin astronaut behind the wheel was worth talking about again—history that I'd lived only vicariously through archived footage and stories told by my grandparents, especially my *avó* Sofia—my father's mother—who'd been glued to the story the day it broke. Her passion for space travel had fueled mine, and I'd held onto every word.

Kytzia snickered, a small smile on her lips. At least I'd managed that. "Cute."

"Sometimes. It comes and goes."

She snorted a laugh, her sombre expression creeping back. "Christmas. I meant the discussion we had at Christmas. Do you remember the promise we made?" Kytzia's glance trailed back down the hall. "Do we still mean it? That decision?" she asked softly, her accent wrapped around her words like a cuddly blanket straight from Auckland.

"Yeah, I remember." How could I forget? We'd talked at length on Christmas Eve, snuggled up close to the window in my room, sharing the same comforter while we stared out into space. As we'd drunk lukewarm apple cider and munched on shortbread and pumpkin pie, we'd reminisced a little too much, falling into a discussion we'd had a million times before: Dath. We were tied together by where we'd been with him, so very little difference in our emotions and how we perceived what went down before he left. Time had not only taken away some of the sting, it'd brought Kytzia and I closer, giving us common ground rooted in the heart.

But this past Christmas, Kytzia had received word that the Alpha Centauri biology crew would dock in a handful of days, and that meant coming face to face with the inevitable, whether we were ready or not.

We wanted to be ready, that much had been made obvious as we'd sat there and talked for hours, me hanging onto every syllable and forcing myself to breathe when I forgot how. We wanted Dath back. Both of us. Regardless of the hurt. Despite whatever lies he thought he'd feed us or how fast and how far he thought he'd have to run before we got the point.

At the end of it all, past every single doubt and reason, we hadn't been able to let go of him—of the idea of the three of us. Maybe we'd been thinking too small back then, when both Kytzia and I asked Dath to choose one of us, but like the ever-expanding universe, our perspective changed with what time threw at us. Maybe *us* was so much bigger than just me and him, or him and Kytzia. Maybe *us* was a whole dimension wider, but we hadn't been able to see it until the last point was in place. Hell, maybe we'd drawn our axes wrong and skewed the entire shape of what we could be.

Either way, we weren't done with him, however done he thought he was with us. Kytzia remained as serious about going steady with him as I did. More than anyone, she understood what I saw in him—why I wanted to fight to keep him. Why I'd stopped having casual flings but never told him, especially when I was afraid of asking him to consider something permanent with me after I'd been the one who suggested casual to begin with.

I hadn't planned on it, not when we'd first met down on the ground. We'd simply exchanged smiles and jokes over really horrible coffee at the station-wide meetings before I bothered asking him out—and subsequently kept asking, because a single date had barely scratched the surface of friendship. I certainly hadn't planned on it when I'd gotten the permanent post here, after a couple years of being bounced from home base to Crosspoint. Things just *happened*, no different than they had with Kytzia. Getting to know Dath, the hours we'd spent together laughing and talking and fooling around, all that time of working through my personal crap with his help, getting my kids to where they needed to be—casual became this tiny little word on the back of an even larger thought. It'd been a wish, a hope, and a chance at something tender that I wanted so deeply.

And he'd thrown it back at me, like I'd feared

he would.

Maybe it wasn't the best timing. Maybe I pushed too far, too late. Would things have been different if I'd asked before then? Would he have chosen differently had he never had a chance to hook up with Kytzia? He'd used my own preference for non-commitment against me, and maybe that was my fault from the beginning, but I thought it'd work. We'd agreed. Dammit, we'd *agreed*.

I just couldn't hold up my end of the bargain.

Meanwhile, Kytzia… She'd had the patience of the saints, taking the pieces of Dath he'd shared with her after he'd given parts of him to me. There'd never been a nasty fight between us, just a quiet understanding she'd gone along with. So for her to turn around and want more—to want to be chosen first—I understood it, I really did. I'd lived that right along with her, just on the opposite side of Dath's bed.

Christmas had put everything into a fresh perspective, with echoes and whispers that maybe the problem was we'd only ever seen the opposite sides of the same bed instead of sharing it.

On Christmas morning, before we'd left Crosspoint for Earth to spend the holiday with our families, Kytzia and I had made a pact: once Dath was back, we'd pursue him together. We'd sealed that promise with a kiss under the prettiest fake mistletoe I could scrounge up…

"scrounge up" being the operative term after someone's marauder bot tried to shred the ever-living fuck out of it.

Kytzia sighed now as we stopped outside of her room. "You remember, but do you mean it still? It wasn't merely us getting caught up in the Chrissy cheer, was it?" She frowned at the door. "It isn't just me?"

"Hey, now." Before she went any further down that line of thought, I hugged her tight and tucked her head against my chest. "Never just you, I promise. It's me, too. I'm still here, *docinho*, still agreeing. And I meant it, every word."

I had, too, though her question was a fair one. Even from a young age, I'd never been one to take shit from other people. Yeah, I was headstrong and stubborn, but I knew who I was. I knew I was worth more than being shat all over. When it came to relationships, I'd do everything I could to make them work; to make sure all parties were happy. But if anyone wanted me to be someone I wasn't, I railed against it, usually quietly, but mostly by walking away—unless they were worth fighting for.

I'd learned that lesson about loyalty and respect early on in life, when the cuts had been deepest, betrayal using regret like a double-edged knife. The worst part? The blow had been dealt by someone I loved, someone I'd looked up to as a kid: my *avô* Alexio, my father's father. I'd been named after him originally, along with my second name, Mackian, to honour my mam's Irish heritage. Growing up, I'd thought my *avô* would never be far from my thoughts, always right there with a kind word and tender gesture to soothe away the fucked-up ills that life threw up.

What a charming, youthful fantasy that had turned out to be, best kept under the bed in a tattered old shoebox with dust bunnies and liquid nitrogen.

I hadn't realized *he'd* be someone I needed safety from until I'd seriously questioned my gender as a teen, searching for more of myself in the feminine threads of who I was. When I was sixteen, I considered legally changing my name to Maria, hoping that would better capture me like a still photo capturing our essence in a single moment. I'd already started to take new pronouns for a test-drive and consider HRT—why not do something about my name, too? Besides, Maria was one of *avó* Sofia's names, and I loved her to the stars and beyond, so it was fitting.

It became a reality when I was eighteen, after I'd realized what an utter asshole my grandfather really was when it came to my life. *My life, my choice,* I'd thought, but not by his books. No, I wasn't to embarrass him by betraying his name—by betraying *him,* even though none of it had anything *to do* with him. The choice was a vicious gauntlet thrown down between us: my happiness or his ultimatums. My security or his rules.

In the end, he'd underestimated just how much his problem wouldn't be mine. Not only was changing my name a means to be more me, it became my way to fight his transphobic bullshit. He couldn't accept who I was? Fine, because I'd given it right on back and smiled all the way through: I dropped his name and was Maria Mackian by the time I started classes at the University of Ottawa, living loud and proud, knowing I'd piss him off just by being me and always getting the upper hand. The rest of my *família* happily accepted the change and told my grandfather to back off, which made it that much more significant.

That had been so long ago, and I still felt the sting of it, the wound carved permanently into my soul and equally unforgettable as the death of my sister, Isabella.

But Dath leaving? That was another stab of regret that pierced just as deeply, a twist of loyalty around a screw that had gone horribly awry. I hadn't even realized it'd gone that far. I hadn't felt the roots of our relationship dig that deep, but when he'd called it quits, I'd felt it harder than I had in a long time. I couldn't help but think he hadn't believed in me enough or trusted my intentions; that there'd been an ultimatum shoved between us I'd completely overlooked. Disbelief had hit me first, followed by the backstab of betrayal, then a need to negotiate our way into something that didn't leave me staring at the back of his ship. Unfortunately, my timing there sucked: by the time I realized what I could've—should've—done, he was already a light year away.

But forgiveness, that came soon after, especially when I realized he was running, scared and overwhelmed, maybe even lying to himself, too, even if it was for all the right reasons. I'd had time to think back, to reconsider our relationship, trying to understand where I'd gone wrong assuming he might want me like I wanted him. Every time, I kept coming up with something more than what he'd left me with. That heartache refused to give up the ghost, reminding me of all the reasons I'd wanted him to stay in the first place.

Dath may have walked away, unable to fight for us, but that didn't mean I wasn't going to toss a *not cancelled* gauntlet into his ridiculously cute face. I'd meant it when I told Kytzia I'd woo him back with her. Absolutely, and with every bit of my heart. I'd forgiven him years ago, especially after discovering for myself why he wouldn't have wanted to leave Kytzia. I'd fight like hell to keep her, so why wouldn't he?

Why couldn't *we*?

"Dath ignoring us isn't going to be an answer

anymore," I whispered, my lips pressed to the top of Kytzia's head, the metal of the crisscrossed bobby pins that kept her bangs back offering a cool touch on my skin. "Not unless he really means it—not because he's trying to spare us or do the right thing, and definitely not if he thinks running is better. He's missing, and we know it. We just need *him* to know it, too."

Kytzia's arms slid around my waist with a quick squeeze. "I'm all for making this year a happy one," she said. "Maybe even get a little payback." I swore her eyes blazed like the sun behind her contacts as she peered up at me, a genuinely mischievous grin blossoming into life. "And I have a *Plan*. Capital P."

Laughing at the images that promise stirred, I kissed her and playfully nipped her lips until she giggled, because heaven help anyone who got in the way of any Kytzia plan that boasted a capital P. The ride alone would be worth every moment.

CHAPTER THREE
Ye Damn Ship

Dath
Wednesday, January 7th

"No, you piece of crap, I *won't* give you my password again," I hissed at the locked door keeping me from my office and lab.

"I'm sorry," the computer in charge of door operations said, "that's not a valid password. You have two attempts left. Please try again or contact an administrator."

"Administrator, my ass," I mumbled, shifting my coffee mug, two tablets, and a container of breakfast leftovers between my hands. Once more, I flattened my palm against the touchpad on the wall, letting it scan my handprint to restart the process all over again. "I'll get you reprogrammed if you don't let me in, useless trash of my—"

"Hey, Dath!" a cheerful voice with a Georgian accent called from behind me: Tamara, one of the RED department's senior geologists I needed to catch up with once I got in the mood to actually be social. The scent of strawberry yogurt and granola swept past as Tamara stopped by my side in the busy corridor of the research department, spoon in one hand and a tall, metal cup in the other. "Need help?" she offered, all smiles, pale green eyes, dark brown skin, and black hair buzzed down to half an inch. Tamara waved her spoon at the wall. "Guess it didn't get the memo, huh?"

"Definitely not the important one," I agreed, sticking my tongue out at the pad as it blinked green and moved onto the voice-activation.

"Please state your name and password," the computer said.

"Ardath Willowford Bellin, hot house potatoes and mash-ups," I answered, rolling my eyes as the door finally unlocked with a click.

Tamara snorted, then choked on a laugh, one hand at her lips. "Jesus, that's a password." She tilted her head to the side, her hand now at her hip, bringing my attention to her charcoal-grey polo shirt and dark blue cargos. "Don't think I've ever heard your full name. It's pretty."

"Thanks." I mustered a tired smile as I pushed open the door. "My parents… All their idea." Yeah, them and their wicked sense of humour, constantly tied up with movies, books, and pop culture. My name had been inspired by fantasy and sci-fi characters they'd loved.

"So I'll see you tomorrow, then? Mission debrief, yeah?" Tamara threw me another smile and gently elbowed my arm. "I hear it's eye-opening and more."

"Oh, yeah, it's side-splitting and hair-pulling—literally, because we skipped right over figurative," I said, driving my hand through the air in a curved line to mimic a plane. "Couldn't do it half-assed, even if we'd tried."

Snickering, Tamara patted my shoulder sympathetically. "Looking forward to it, kid." She cocked a brow at the door and nodded. "Don't work too hard now that you're back, 'kay? Keep it real, but don't push it."

Mm, like my therapist told me yesterday at our first session. Kind of like everyone else had been saying to me and my crew ever since we got back. It'd be annoying if it weren't sweet.

"Thanks, Tams. Will do." I grinned and waved her off with a wink, pushing into the lab and closing the door behind me. The botany labs were divided into two sections: benches, fridges, racks, and everything for experiments were to my right, split into multiple rooms by glass walls, while our offices, which were mostly solid white walls with glass top halves and full glass fronts, were to my left. Across from the run of five offices were a meeting space and a big, black square table with ten dark violet chairs settled around it.

I wasn't the only one here: Farah leaned over a bench in one of the labs, the soft sounds of a centrifuge spinning out as she studied a striking yellow and teal star-seed plant I'd brought back from Alpha Centauri. Zsuzsi was in her office on the corner, not far from where I stood, vidchatting by the looks of it as I caught sight of the consistent swish of her short blonde ponytail through the window. I heard a couple more voices, though I couldn't see their owners from the doorway: Alonzo's deep voice carried into the open space from near his office on the other side of mine, combined with Vena's soft singing as ze slid what sounded like glass tubes into a fridge at the other end of the lab. All in all, a fully-functioning morning here at—I squinted at my tablet—1000 hours.

Fuck. Late again. Third time this week, and it was only day three since I'd been back. The doctors had said this might happen, including Therapist Hannah, who'd assured me it was normal, so 'don't sweat it.'

Okay, great advice, don't get me wrong, but I'd sweat a lot less if work wasn't being such a massive pain in my everything. There was *so much* to do before I went home—enough that it could take three weeks to get through it all instead of the single week or so I'd hoped for. I needed to complete as much as possible before I left, reducing the amount of work I'd have when I returned, even if that meant delaying my departure date.

With a resigned sigh as I faced the ultimate truth, I trudged towards my office, next door to

Zsuzsi's. My office wasn't very big or spectacular, but it did the trick. My white U-shaped desk sat in the middle of the room, the shortest side parallel with the door, in front of a black chair that was turned a little to the left. One laptop was off to the right on the desktop, under the overhead cabinets. My second laptop waited on the shorter part of the desk, facing the doorway and wall cabinets filled with hard drives containing records, research, and the raw notes from my lab work. Tablets with reference materials and a dozen hardcover books took up half of the remaining space, along with a vase of common daisies and tricolour chrysanthemums my team had kindly placed on my desk as a homecoming gift. The dozen posters I'd hung on the walls were triptychs and collages of photos I'd taken of the old-growth forests and giant sequoias in British Columbia, the last remaining marshes in Ontario, the treeline up north, and gardens across the country, especially in Québec and along the east coast from Nova Scotia to Newfoundland. They were colourful reminders of home; attempts to tether me to where I'd been and where I'd eventually return once I grew tired of being out here… or when here was tired of me.

Heart-heavy and barreled over with a sudden wave of fatigue, I slipped around my desk and sank into my chair, discarding the tablets, mug, and leftovers onto the desktop. The fatigue came and went, usually as quickly as it did now, along with a dull headache that had played peek-a-boo every day for the last week. I'd managed to find time to meditate and ground as best I could, and my stomach was thrilled to be spoiled, but I couldn't shake the rest of the *off* feeling I had. The doctors said it was because I'd been away for so long, and the stress of re-acclimating came with its own challenges, but that it'd ease with time, attention to self-care, and everything that was supposed to be good for me. For now, I needed to accept it and move forward.

Ugh, forward. Straight into the odious beast that was my To Do list.

Debrief tomorrow, eleven hundred hours, I reminded myself, snatching the smaller black personal tablet off my desk to swipe the screen. I zipped through my calendars and lists. *Finish unloading my gear. Take inventory of what we took to AC and figure out what needs replacing and recycling. Save whatever we can reuse.* Taking a swig of my warm coffee, I continued swiping through the list. *Plant the cuttings I brought back so Farah and Alonzo can babysit them while I'm gone. Get our data into the network and set up the preliminary analyses, then tweak the algorithms so they'll run while I'm off—Zsuzsi's got that handled, thankfully. Still have to do all the notes, though. Give her an idea of what she's looking at.* I squinted at the screen, frowning at my own poor spelling brought on by late-night ramblings. *'Exrcze'… Dammit, should've just said 'gym.' And 'Tannah - Esess's'?*

"Dafuq was I thinking when I wrote this?" I shook my head until I realized the note in question was a reminder to talk to my therapist about seeing a psychologist at the ground station while I was home. Damn shorthand.

The last item stunned me silent, even as Zsuzsi's joyful laughter drifted over from where she stood talking to Alonzo outside her door:

Upgrades and patches to our tech and Sleipnir, particularly all comms, systems, and warp drive—especially if it's finally been pushed to six times the speed of light like I remember someone talking about before we left.

Upgrades.

My ship.

Mack.

Shit.

Had I promised myself to stop thinking about Mack? No, because I wanted to actually achieve something while I was back and breaking promises seemed like a bad first step. But had I *tried* not to think about Mack? Had I *tried* not to think about Kytzia, with her being all up in Mack's personal space and enjoying the affection between them?

Gods, yes and yes. Tried and failed miserably, over and over.

I'd spent the last four years trying to

convince myself I wasn't in love with either of them, but some lies you can't make real, no matter how hard you try. No matter how much you needed to believe the lie.

Kind of like the lie that, if I kept avoiding them, I'd never have to deal with anything face to face.

Talk about being delusional. Setting aside the tablet and coffee, I turned on the laptop to my left, then signed into the station network and found the service schedule the mech bay maintained to keep everyone else informed of what they were up to. The mechanics I'd talked to said they'd take a look at my ship and give me an update by the end of the week, especially if they couldn't get the work done by the end of January.

Funny, because looking at the schedule right now, the *Sleipnir* had been knocked down the list of jobs—*with an ETA of completion in mid-fucking-March*—or the Earth equivalent of it, anyway. And the asterisk beside it? Oh, *great.* "Jobs marked with an asterisk could take longer to be completed, due to supplier times and other circumstances," or so the footnote said.

The hell? *Sleipnir* needed maintenance. Routine checks. Maybe the upgrades if I was super lucky and they felt extra giving within the short timeframe, but I'd told them I could wait for the fancy stuff until I got back from Earth. I only needed the basics, even if the outside looked like a golf ball. But *ten weeks or more*?!

Oh, they were *so* hearing about this. That and I wanted to know why no one bothered to text me about the change, considering the time stamp on the service update said 0700 this morning.

Leaving my coffee and tablet on the desk, I stormed off to the bay to demand what was up with their what-the-fuckery. It was too early in the day to get bad news and let it fester without answers.

The mech bay was a loud, giant entity labeled as deck one and deck two, though really, it was more like twelve decks put together with most of their walls and floors torn out. The hands-on work was done on the lower deck, with the vessels moored and mechanics moving about around them, tools powered on and making a racket that killed my head with more drilling than a dentist. If a ship or other vessel couldn't fit in the space, they kept it docked to the station's exterior. Thankfully the *Sleipnir* was a modest research ship that fit into the bay just fine.

The upper deck was actually a partial deck with offices, a staff lounge, and the service desk, though the shouts and sharp metallic noise from the lower deck carried up and over as though there weren't any floor between them at all. Then again, it was only half a floor, connected to the lower deck by a staircase and multiple lifts.

The deck above—deck three—that was where Mack's office was, along with the other mechanical engineers, who tended to move throughout the station. Mostly they haunted the halls and bays with new ideas, building their models and running simulations, working on project after project. Mack was in charge of it all, managing everything and overseeing new solutions, among other things, that could be sent to Earth to keep pushing their tech forward.

I marched up to the service desk, the first thing I saw when I stepped out of the lift and into the hall. The long, white desk in its boxy kiosk was occupied by two staff members, one of whom was engrossed in a conversation with someone enquiring about navigation systems. The second staff member—a young redhead with shaggy hair and a bright blue shirt with grey and white stripes—smiled as I approached. *Dany*, or so their little black name tag said.

"Morning," Dany greeted, chipper and genuinely polite. "What can I help you with?"

"My ship." I gritted my teeth, not wanting to take anything out on someone who looked like they'd just stepped out of Frosh Week for a non-alcoholic beer with their roommates because that's all they could get legally. "The *Sleipnir*. I need to talk to someone about why it's been bumped to the middle of—"

"*Dath?*"

Fuuuuuuuu…

Mack.

Right there, stepping out of an office to my left and stopping so close to the wall I wondered if xe was going to fall against it or bolt in the opposite direction.

"Dath," Mack said again, xir heavy, black work boots clunky on the floor as xe moved towards me slowly. Mack must've had meetings today, considering xe wore dark blue cargo pants with a tiny grey tablet in the pocket by xir left knee and an un-tucked, navy-blue button-up shirt over a black t-shirt, the long sleeves rolled up to Mack's elbows while the silver cap of a pen peeked out of xir shirt pocket. Once again, what remained of Mack's hair was pulled back into a ponytail that hung over xir shoulder, and dark eyeliner ringed xir eyes, along with a hint of dusky grey eye shadow. Two sets of silver studs were in Mack's ears, joined by a set of small silver hoops. "Hey, stranger."

It shouldn't have been difficult to respond to that, but like hell could I say anything even *close* to a simple word right now.

Mack stopped two feet away from me and smiled softly—hesitantly—almost as if xe read my mind. "*Tudo bem*? Is everything okay?"

No, everything was *not* okay, but fuck if I could remember what *okay* was or how to communicate it.

"Shit—" I cleared my throat, all my fire gone. "I mean *ship*. Mine. Bumped?"

Mack's face fell, the gentle smile gone as xe turned to Dany. "I've got this." Xe turned back to me, one arm extended towards the series of black chairs lining the hallway several feet away. "Come on. Let's chat over here."

I followed without so much as a second thought.

So much for avoiding xem.

We stopped at the seats in the middle, though neither of us sat down, even as people passed us in the corridor. It was just as well: had we been alone, I didn't know what would've come out of my mouth.

Mack offered me another smile, this one apologetic. "I'm sorry," xe said, leaning into me before catching xir breath and falling back a step as though needing a moment to regroup. "There's been… an issue. I was going to find you when you got off work this afternoon and tell you, but since you're here now…" Mack cleared xir throat, hands jammed into xir pockets as xe shrugged xir shoulders forward. "The crew was looking at your ship last night and this morning, diagnosing everything. They were poking around, checking the systems, all of it routine."

With a sigh, Mack took another step back. "Thing is, one of them poked a bit too much, things sparked, and your ship—" Mack winced.

"—*Sleipnir* caught fire, and I'm so bloody sorry. He got fried and busted up pretty bad inside."

What? Just *what* was I supposed to say to *that*?

Fried. Busted. Those were words for eggs, *not my ship*.

"It's going to take time to restore him, make him all nice and safe again. New problems to fix, new parts to get." Mack sucked in a breath and twisted the Iron Ring on the little finger of xir left hand, a rough-edged, stainless steel ring xe always wore. Once upon a few years ago, Mack had told me about its significance and The Ritual of the Calling of an Engineer, all of it so very solemn and steeped in tradition. Whenever Mack was nervous or anxious, especially about work, xe fiddled with it, bringing xem back to the oaths of that tradition and clearing xir thoughts. The fact xe fussed with it now, with me... I wasn't too sure how to feel about that. "It's messed up, and I'm sorry, Dath. I've been pissed since I found out. I'll make them refurb the whole damn thing, no matter their whining. It'll take a couple months, but he'll be practically brand new when you get him back."

I couldn't help it: I groaned, all of my disappointment pouring out in the open. I should've known the Goddess Brigit would test me and my resolve to get home for Imbolc—or maybe I had the whole damn Celtic pantheon to thank for this. Hell, maybe even the Norse pantheon, too, because Loki and Odin had always loved dancing around my family like a Heathen binary star that kept us on our toes.

"I just wanted to go home," I mumbled before I realized I did it. *Dammit*, I added silently, feeling my face flush.

"When?" Mack asked softly, leaning into me, brown gaze all sympathetic and concerned and… and something else I wasn't anywhere near deserving of.

Wait, hold up. Mack hadn't paused there, just asked, and that look… I'd gotten that look several times before, when things were good between us. That—none of this—it wasn't anything like I'd expected. Where was the pissed-off ex? Why weren't we parting ways? I'd left Mack behind, yet xe was pissed about my gutted ship?

"At the end of the month," I answered quietly, too confused to do anything else. "A little before then, actually."

It all happened so quickly: Mack reaching out to touch me, only to retract at the last second and curl xir fingers into a fist at xir side, as if touching me committed some sort of terrible act.

"There's still time to work it out," xe said with a weak smile. "He might get fixed sooner than we think. Sometimes parts don't take long to come around, or we miraculously find something we hid somewhere—any number of things. And me, I'm a glutton for punishment, you know that. I'm usually in the bay after-hours, anyway, so I could poke my head under the hatches and install some things. Failing that..." Mack took a deep breath and stepped close enough that I caught the warm autumn scent of xir aftershave, its spicy cinnamon and nutmeg fragrance balanced with the sweetness of vanilla and apples. "I could take you down myself. Be your own personal escort."

A statement, not a question.

A very *pointed* statement, one that screamed *Imagine all the things we could do* instead of *Here's me burying you in the bowels of space for breaking my heart.*

Sweet Brigit and the Mórrígan, I think I may've slipped into some kind of alternate reality. Just one inch, maybe two, and my lips would've touched Mack's. The slightest head tilt and I could've offered all sorts of apologies out there in the hall. Would Mack push me away if I tried?

Except that was a privilege I hadn't earned, and this was becoming really awkward, really fast.

I should've asked about Mack's kids, Siobhan and Tiago, especially since I'd helped Mack with their university concerns. I should've asked about Mack's parents and siblings. I should've asked about Kytzia, how long they'd been seeing each other, and how she was faring with all of her family troubles. I should've said a lot of things, including a simple, "Thank you," which was all I would've needed to say.

Instead, I choked out a strangled, "*I can't,*" and ran away.

Because being in a small space with Mack? Heading down to Earth *with Mack*? That was a fear I wasn't ready to confront, especially if it ended up somewhere we couldn't come back from. If I wanted off this station, I'd be better off taking my chances with one of the old junkers the mechanics tinkered with every so often and praying to every god in the pantheon that I made it alive. Because why the fuck should Mack do *anything* for me? I was the one who owed Mack, and I still didn't know how to pay up. Just how broke would I have to be before I finally figured any of it out?

CHAPTER FOUR
Follow the Lizard

Dath
Friday, January 9th

Somewhere between my library of alternative tunes playing quietly and a wannabe vat of over-sweetened coffee, I was trying hard to ignore the fact it was my first Friday night back and I was still working. Somehow, data and classification forms had wormed their way into the priority list over TGIF activities, most of which included kicking back in one of the lounges and just... I didn't know, really. I tended to people-watch more than anything, finding contentment in conversation and classic B-movies.

In some ways, being here in my office wasn't too far off from that, though I drew the line at alien plants that suddenly sprang to life and started chasing me around the lab, trying to suck my brains out. I'd already lived that with a few critters. I'd met my quota...

Damn, how twisted was it that I wanted to tack a "for now" onto that thought?

"You lied to me," I told my coffee, as if it alone was supposed to make me feel like I was fitting back into daily life.

Retaliation was swift: the moment I took another swig, I partially missed the lip of the mug and lukewarm coffee dribbled down my chin, drops hitting my desk and leaving tiny, muddy brown puddles on the pristine white.

"Okay, okay, I take it back," I mumbled, wiping my chin with the back of my hand. "Keep your beans together." Glancing into the lit hallway and at the empty offices on either side of me, I pulled down the long sleeve of my black jacket and used it to clean the desk. Between me and a drink that had the talent to fight back, tonight was getting longer. Though I was hoping with everyone else gone, I could breeze through these numbers and forms and get a taste of some sort of cooler before I headed to bed. Or a shot of vodka, maybe two. Crosspoint imported the good stuff, so really…

My headache sucker punched my skull, apparently offended with my drink choice.

"Oww!" I winced and rubbed my temple. The ache had made a permanent home in my head this last week, kicking things up a notch now with jabbing pains. I'd been trying to *not* make it worse, even wearing contacts instead of my glasses to keep the weight off, but I'd definitely failed somewhere. Frowning at my coffee, I set the mug aside. Maybe the onslaught of caffeine had something to do with it. I'd switch to decaf tomorrow and rummage through the cafeteria's selection of herbal teas. For extra measure, I turned off the music and let silence take over.

I needed to focus on getting things done… while simultaneously holding back from stalking the mech bay's schedule to see if the *Sleipnir* had been bumped up at all, even by a day or so, or if there were any service notes. Anything at all that could give me some hope.

Or at least the sort that didn't put me in close quarters with someone I wanted to be more than close with—someone who should've been keying my metaphorical car, not offering to take me home.

And that, *that* was why I loved Mack. Always the person I'd never expected, always so caring, always so… Mack.

So then why was I sitting here, kicking myself when I should've been apologizing for choosing so poorly the first time around? I was apparently repeating the same mistake now. Some kind of door had been opened, but I was glued to the spot, staring into a void of questions. Even if I stepped over that threshold to see where the path led, where did that leave Kytzia? There was no going back, I knew that, but how could we go forward when they couldn't trust me or my bad decisions, however well-meaning I wanted to be?

Gods, I sucked at being a boyfriend even

when I wasn't one.

"Imbolc," I muttered, the keys of my laptop clickety-clacking harder as I tried to move on while struggling to spell another ridiculously long Latin name. "Family. Grove. Friends. I'm good at those. Stick to those."

Yeah... Problem was I didn't want to, and the long-shot thought of sharing any portion of my vacation with Mack sounded a little too good.

A soft click sounded somewhere in the lab, followed by a second, louder noise, almost as though someone had opened a door and tried closing it as fast as they could without being caught.

Scowling, I stood up and glanced through the glass half of Zsuzsi's office to the entrance into the botany suite. Still closed. I swept my gaze over what I could see of the labs, meeting room, and other offices.

"Just you and me," I finally said to the laptop, frowning at the cursor blinking in the half-finished *Species* field.

Wrong. So very wrong.

We weren't alone.

Something was here, whirring away with faint mechanical noises and... tiny steps... that sounded like a cat in need of a manicure?

The. Hell.

Mug in hand, I shot around my desk to my office door, foolishly intending to fend off the mechanical beast with the least threatening object there. *Yeah, you come on, thing.* I peered into the hallway. *Let's see you.*

A small shadow loomed across the hall, the whirring coming closer. Legs followed, then the head, the body, and the—the—

Lizard?

"*Qu'est-ce que* fuck?" I shouted, then clapped my hand over my mouth. The lizardbot continued towards me, its shiny burnt-orange and pearl-white body painted with sunshine-yellow and glossy black stripes, the pattern something between a tiger and a bee. Its body wasn't any bigger than my work boot, but its tail extended behind it by about half a foot, swinging back and forth. Emerald-green eyes flickered, the glow reflecting off the glass wall of Zsuzsi's office, and its tongue—yep, there was one, the neon-green tip hanging out of its mouth.

Stunned, my brain still stuck on the *lizard* part, I was thrown when the thing stopped in the middle of the hall.

Once Lizardbot started climbing the glass, I was *done.*

I booked it into my office and slammed the door. Give me zombies. Give me triffids. Give me roaches. I was drawing the line at unannounced animal bots that climbed vertical surfaces.

Lizardbot kept scaling the wall, unfazed by

the fact that I leaned against the door, heart palpitating a speed metal drum track as I glared at the methodical movement of its narrow orange and yellow legs. I couldn't see any of the circuits or wires inside, but maybe if I stared at it long enough…

The damn thing curved its way in my direction, as if it knew hiding behind a glass door was the worst thing I could've chosen to do. Little bloody menace. *Click, click, click* on the glass, eyes still glowing, tail still moving—well, drooping, sort of.

No doubt I'd ask myself later why I didn't just grab the thing and find the off switch. Maybe because I was still that person that screamed bloody murder when a spider dropped in front of me in the shower. Or maybe I could chalk it up to homecoming jitters. Yeah, solid explanation, that.

Either way, I breathed a sigh of relief when Lizardbot finally stopped. On my door. Stuck right along the centre line, two inches from my face, practically staring at me as if it had eyes in the front of its head. I could see where the tiny screws were and the suggestions of panels…

Ping! Ping, ping, ping!

I jumped, rattling both the door and the bot. Damn thing was nearly as loud as a fire alarm.

Ping! Ping… Pingpingpingpingpingpingping.

"Okay!" I yelled back, then opened the door slowly, careful not to bap Lizardbot off. It stuck well, whoever had designed it. They were also going to hear about this... and clean the smudges off the glass.

Lizardbot's mouth opened, neon tongue sliding out ever so slightly. "Message for you, Dath," it announced in a smooth, oddly childlike voice that was lightly distorted, jaws working as though it really could speak. Its eyes glowed brighter as it continued. "A game, should you choose to accept it. Ever scavenger hunted?"

I whimpered. Gods, no. Yes, I had. No, I didn't want—

"That's not really an answer, Dath."

It paused in wait. After scolding me.

I hated tech sometimes.

"Yeah, I have," I answered, hating that even more. "Why?"

"Come on." Lizardbot snapped its mouth shut and moved, legs pivoting and manoeuvring it down the door.

"Just so you know," I said, "I'm totally unconvinced."

"Don't need you to be convinced," Lizardbot said, clicking down onto the floor. "Just intrigued. Unless you really get off on data input and taxonomy."

Huh. Other than having crude cheekiness, it knew what I'd been up to. Interesting.

"Right. So, is this your regular Friday night, then?" I asked, daring to follow as Lizardbot walked down the hall.

"Dath, don't be ridiculous. I'm logged as a non-sentient entity."

"That I'm talking to."

"Exactly." Lizardbot paused, one front foot raised as it twisted its head to the left. "So, who's not convinced now?"

Point.

"Fine, I'll play." I motioned to the lab. "Go on, get scavenging."

"No, that's all you, Dath. I'm just the messenger," Lizardbot's chipper voice told me, tail dragging across the floor as it moved onwards. Thin lines of tiny, orange LED lights transected the tail at varying intervals, the widest set two inches apart.

We reached the entrance to the labs before Lizardbot turned towards me, doing what looked like its best impression of a miniature monster. Funny enough, it finally occurred to me that I was still holding my coffee and could've splashed it all over the bot, claiming a natural disaster killed it…

"Don't do it, Dath. I'm expensive, and you can't afford me."

I snorted. "You've got a mouth on you, you know that?"

"Yup, tongue, too. Can't blow raspberries, though."

"Because there's something to aspire to."

I swore the thing would've smiled if it could've. "You have no idea." Lizardbot stalked towards me four steps and stopped, eyes flashing. "First instruction: Sugar, spice, and everything you might crave lays before you. Where am I?"

Up shit creek without a paddle?

We stared at each other in the silence.

"I have a feeling you're not thinking, Dath." Lizardbot's tail swiped the floor, tapping it quietly. "Try. Be adventurous."

"I had four years of *adventure*, thanks. I'm fresh out."

"Try curiosity, then. Unless that's completely packed a sad, too?"

Packed a sad.

Packed a sad.

A small smile tugged at my lips before I could stop it, even as my stomach flipped and danced. *Got ya, Kytzia.*

How many times had she said that when we'd been together, whenever something or someone was broken or just generally being moody? Gods, I loved when the Kiwi vernacular slipped into whatever she was saying, usually while I was too busy listening to her voice to really notice. But I noticed now. *That's* how Lizardbot knew what I'd been doing in my office: Kytzia knew tech and hacking well enough to wreak havoc on most people if she'd really wanted to.

More importantly, she was here. She wanted to play.

Who was I to disappoint?

Granted, I was confused, ready to throw up, and terrified of where this would lead, but disappoint her… I'd done that already, and *fuck* was I tired of it. Mostly I was thrown by the effort, too surprised to say no. First Mack, now Kytzia. What was this?

"Curiosity it is," I said softly, placing my mug against the wall beside the doorjamb. "Sugar and spice, you say? Well, then, to the cafeteria we go."

I'd done my fair share of scavenger hunts as a kid, so this one didn't worry me. Once I opened the door, Lizardbot clicked its way out into the hallway and waited, content to leisurely follow me to the lift. Thankfully no one was in the lift when we boarded and went down to deck four—the less I had to explain as to why I was with a robotic reptile, the better.

We stepped out of the lift, immediately greeted by soft pop music and the smell of popcorn. I stood at the cafeteria doors, Lizardbot at my feet, and stared into the dimly lit room. A group of about thirty people sat off to the right side of the room, watching a concert being projected onto the wall and singing along when they weren't commenting on the singer's elaborate outfit and dance moves.

"Down here."

I gazed at Lizardbot. "Yes?"

"Second instruction: But look back to where

you've been, get perspective. See where you want to go."

"You're all business, huh?" I muttered, mulling the clue over.

"Says the guy working on a Friday night."

A solid two-pointer, that one. *Look back to where you've been. Perspective.* Did it mean Alpha Centauri? Earth? *See where you want to go.* Earth, so very much Earth, but it was more than that. Mostly I was stuck on the *perspective* bit, for more reasons than just this game. I was missing a hundred things, I knew that, especially the part that explained why I wasn't being ignored like I'd done to Kytzia and Mack. Was that even going to be a part of this exercise: finding out *why* they were giving me a second chance? Why it *felt* like I was getting another go at what I'd given up? I swore I was seeing all the signs and reading them right, but maybe I was only seeing what I wanted—

"Observation deck," I said, turning on my heel. Our next step was deck twenty-two, though I didn't venture far onto the deck. There were couples present, gathered near the expanse of windows that went around the entire circular deck. The panoramic view offered a glimpse of Mars and whatever other cosmic bodies were outside, and everyone on the deck was looking out into the darkness, taking quiet moments to themselves to whisper and watch our solar system merely exist.

I'd done the same thing with Kytzia, more than once joining her here after a long work week, when we'd both needed to find peace, unwind, and take a moment to remember why we were at Crosspoint. We'd shared stories of home, speaking so quietly as if we'd wake someone way out here in this unfamiliar orbit. I'd held her close, needing that comfort of home and finding it in her calm. This was where she'd first told me about what was happening with her family—their woes, aches, losses, and her fears about being here instead of there. We'd stared into the depths of the solar system for hours that night, talking through what it meant to live, survive, and push forward even when everything else fell apart.

So being here now…

Not wanting to disturb anyone, I picked Lizardbot up under one arm and retreated into the lift, closing the door behind us. Maybe if I didn't look, it'd lessen the sting of what the deck took me back to. "I take it that was right?"

"Well, it certainly wasn't left."

"You suck."

"Actually, no. No suction. Didn't have the parts."

I tipped my head back and rolled my eyes. "*Correct*. Was it *correct*, then?"

"Yeah, so here's number three: Because even when the weight of the world is heavy, and you wish you could float away."

Seriously? Was she trying to give me this on a silver platter? I could have either kissed her for it or shaken my head and asked for a harder clue. Considering I'd never expected any of this, I wasn't about to push my luck.

"Zero-grav chamber," I said, pressing 3 on the keypad, all too happy to leave behind the memories still clinging to the observation deck like ghosts romancing each other. We zipped down to the engineering department, where we were met with dark, silent hallway. Still holding Lizardbot, I strolled through the corridor. There wasn't much to see here, mostly doors to offices and labs, all of them closed. As we passed Mack's office, I closed my eyes and let my feet do all the work, even turning my head away. Whatever this game was, it couldn't end well, as cute as Kytzia was. The choices were still there. The lies, too. They wouldn't be erased or forgotten. But forgiven? Could Kytzia and Mack *do* forgiving? Was that what this was: an exercise in earning that trust and forgiveness? A way to say we could be friends again? Had I earned that grace?

We stopped by the entrance to one of the zero-G chambers on the deck. Snorting, I couldn't help but hear Mack's voice in my head. Mack used xe pronouns, though xe'd answer to almost any pronoun—*almost* being the key word. While Mack tended to be laid back and fun-loving in most circumstances, if anyone were to ever take the derogatory and insulting route with xem, I swore they'd wished they were seriously dead. More than once, Mack had said xe'd opt for throwing the offending asshole into the nearest zero-G chamber with a litre of bodily fluids and, "let that shit sort itself out," a fate I heartily supported.

Soft laughter tumbled out of me, memories pulling it out one breath after another. I loved when Mack talked dirty and took no disrespect from anyone. And heaven forbid someone get cute with Mack's name. Anyone who decided that "Mack the Knife" was an appropriate way to address Mack would probably get a wrench thrown at their head. I still didn't know if anyone here had tried.

"Ready for instruction four?"

The tiny voice rattled me, partially because I'd been deep in thought; partially because for the first time, the bot spoke quietly. "Yeah, sure."

"You never know what beautiful things have been growing around you."

Golden platter. She was giving me these on a golden platter, and I loved her for it, because she was sending me to one of my most favourite places on the station.

"Greenhouse," I said, almost rushing to the lift. At what point I'd picked up my pace, wanting to race to the end of this game and see what happened, I didn't know. My brain was still somewhere in my office, wondering why a talking robot breaking into my lab freaked me out.

That was likely fear, I suspected, putting up a boundary between reality and denial. Though maybe the reality was something to be denied, especially if it couldn't end the way I hoped.

Though at what point had I started hoping? That was the truer question. I'd spent four years resigned to the fate I'd chosen. To have all of that spun around on its head without a word from me…

As we returned to sixth deck, I toyed with my Awen pendant, barely aware that I did it at all. I hadn't meant the choice I'd made, hadn't wanted it, but I couldn't take any of it back. Not without opening every wound that much wider and letting them bleed. I'd spent a long time licking my wounds shut, so this—whatever *this* was—I could only pray that hope waited at the end. I wanted to believe, all that wishing-on-a-star bit coming to mind. I'd wished on a lot of stars. I'd even seen four of them up close. But wishes were many and this reality was one. At what point did they become one in the same?

After the lift, I wandered the corridor to the greenhouse where we kept my finds from Alpha Centauri. I didn't go in, choosing instead to stare through the glass doors to the multi-coloured plants that had newly taken up residence. They'd grow, or so we hoped, and we'd study them during the entire process, teasing out as much knowledge as we could. These plants were nothing like the ones at home, their textures, tastes, and biology as unique to them as they were to their planets. They were everything I'd hoped to find; everything I'd wanted to study. I wanted to get to know them, to love them, to understand them. I wanted to see the world as they did and feel their place within it. They brought light years of universe that much closer, connecting Earth to its intra-galactic cousins through the living. It was one existence connected to another through life itself, both fragile and strong, and I'd cherish that for the rest of my life. The World Tree had more than one face, and I'd been humbled to gaze upon another one of them.

"Ready for your last instruction?" Lizardbot asked.

"Yes." Hugging Lizardbot close, I continued staring into the greenhouse.

"Take a moment of rest and think on it. You'll know where to find us."

I frowned at Lizardbot. "That's it?"

Lizardbot said nothing, just blinked.

"Oh, sure, *now* you check out." Rest, thoughts, finding… That rest bit sounded like an excellent idea. I'd forgotten about my headache until now, but it came back with a roaring vengeance. Yeah, maybe rest was a good plan. I needed to take a guess at where the last stop was, anyway, so what better than my quarters?

When we got there, I stopped, unable to mentally get over the package lying against my door. Wrapped in orange satin bows and tin foil, the package was small and flat, a message written on the top in black marker:

Something to think on. (P.S. George will turn himself off) <3

Just like that, Lizardbot George powered down, eyes losing their glow as George's tail drooped against my hip.

Saddened by the loss, I picked up the package and entered my quarters. I set George on my bed, then took a breath and ripped into the tin foil.

I sucked in a second breath until it hurt, held it.

This was more complicated than I'd realized.

A silver frame sat in my hand, engraved with roses, lilies, and what looked like cornflowers, but it was the digital photo that stabbed me from gut to heart: a picture of me with Mack and Kytzia, standing in front of a copse of trees in autumn, all three of us together, *there*, in a way we'd never been. The source photos were good ones, I'd give Kytzia that. We all looked happy, even if the picture was fake.

What it suggested, though… The photo said a lot of things, none of which I could make sense of right then, not properly. I couldn't process it beyond what I was supposed to do with it, which was stare endlessly at our smiles, our postures, whose arms were around whom. I was in the middle of them, the interpretation there easy to grasp, even if it seemed impossible in my head. Kytzia's arms were wrapped around my waist, with me leaning into Mack.

How I wanted that picture to be real. I'd wish upon our sun a million times for one single chance for it to come true.

Sinking onto my bed, then onto the floor, I stared at the photo, unable to let their gazes go. I didn't know what to do now, how I was supposed to play with this box of *very* complex emotions Kytzia had handed me. I just knew I didn't want to let it go.

CHAPTER FIVE
Resistance, Meet Phase Two

Kytzia Polović
Tuesday, January 13th

Four days later and we still hadn't heard from Dath—hadn't had any indication of the gift we'd left him—and that hurt, even more than the fact he hadn't come to us at all since returning to Crosspoint. The latter I understood, considering how we'd left things, but not to get any response after we'd reached out, trying to tell him we weren't angry anymore? How many ways could we be rejected? It felt like someone had thrown a 404 Not Found error on this entire situation. For all I knew, it was more of a 403 Forbidden: more of a *get off my back forever and always, mate* than *I'm not ready for this yet—give me time*.

Still, pushing him wouldn't work out any nicer, I was certain of that much. If he wanted time, I'd give him that. I'd leave him to his space. For now. At least until I talked to Mack.

Another sigh slipped out, resigned and knackered, and frankly, I just didn't care. It was after 1900 hours and my brain was fried like tires on lava. For being a Tuesday, the whole day had felt like an extension of Monday, with moments where I swore déjà vu smacked me so bloody hard. Gah, *people*. Working with systems went a lot smoother when the human element was removed.

Robots. Give me robots. I folded my arms onto my desk and laid my head on them, looking over my office, telling myself I should get my arse out of the chair and out the door. So sad that I was almost too tired to do that. The office was nice enough, considering I'd done what I could to make her right. Wasn't more than a shoebox of a space, really, despite that *upgraded from a storage closet* flavour most of the IT offices on the station had.

At least this space was mine, colourful with an appropriate amount of cheer that bordered on unprofessional, or maybe crossed the line altogether. New Year's hadn't ended—it'd merely migrated to my L-shaped desk, the blue and silver foil banners and party favours joining the red and green streamers from Christmas, draped around my desk and across the cabinets in the overhead. I may have brought back one too many decorations from home, pushing interior design to this side of gaudy with the metallic purple and gold balls and miniature Santas, but whatever. Happy was happy. Bits of home were bits of home. Forget style when you could be comfy.

The rest of the room was slightly more subdued: while my desk was pushed towards the back of the office, cabinets and a cupboard of manuals took over even more space along the wall to my right and at the front of the office by the door. A pair of black chairs sat to the left, accompanied by a box of black cords and USB drives I'd eventually do something with.

Tomorrow. Think about it tomorrow. My stomach agreed, its gurgling difficult to ignore. I frowned at the laptop. Mack should've shown up by now.

"Probably in mech bay," I murmured, shutting down my laptop. If Mack wasn't lost in some hands-on project, letting off steam by working through physical problems, xe'd be in xir office, sorting things for tomorrow. We'd gotten used to each other's routines, the quirks and habits, and all the little things that made a person who they were. We could read each other most of the time and had a feel for how we'd handle things, separately and together. So far, this issue with Dath… it wasn't so much an issue as it was a test in patience and determination, mostly on our end. We might've been ignored up to now, but we'd take another go at it, still holding onto that team spirit. If Dath didn't want to be part of that team…

I pushed up, grabbed my dark blue pullover from the back of my chair, and left the office, closing the glass door behind me. I needed to keep pushing the bad thoughts away, keep telling them to run along, because I'd had enough of despair and its nasty friends. Between Mack, the doctors, and my older bro, Peter, I'd managed to curb away from depression these last couple years, corralling it into a place I could deal with for now, but the years before that had still happened. The bad days were still bad, but fewer than they'd been when Dath left for Alpha C.

Stopped in the doorway of the IT Systems department suite, I glanced over the darkened offices and cluttered desks in the centre before flicking out the lights and locking down the double doors. A few steps and I was in the lift, feeling like I'd taken a breath of relief. Sometimes the best decision of the day was just getting out of there.

Had that been what Dath felt when he'd dumped me and Mack? That deep breath? As much as I wanted to believe his goodbye had been a lie, I wondered if it had been more than that—if it was me or something I could've done differently. Mack assured me it was xem that'd pushed Dath too far, but my past hated being left out of the equation.

I sighed and slipped into my pullover as the lift descended, then crossed my arms and tugged the pullover tight across my chest and powder-blue t-shirt. Heaps had gone on since I'd been transferred from ECHO ground station to Crosspoint six years ago, most of it crammed into the last five years—or just over two and a half years in Mars time, an illusion I took comfort in on days I sorely needed optimism. For the time he'd been here, Dath had helped me cope with life aboard the station. He'd been exactly what I needed, when I'd needed him: a soundboard, a shoulder to leak mascara on, and the goofball who'd bring me chicken soup and hot chips, then queue up romantic comedies in my room and watch them with me, tossing proverbial tomatoes at the screen and debating the worst pick-up lines in existence.

We'd had fun, even when my little part of Earth smashed apart without me there to piece it back together. My parents' graphics design company going bankrupt surprised us all, followed by their house going into foreclosure, then my father's stroke that left Mum and Peter scrambling to not only find appropriate accommodations, but also adequate healthcare. Not long after they'd barely sorted that, my younger bro, Kasper, came home from his last military tour missing one of his legs while half of the other was paralyzed, roughing up life for him, his wife, and their daughter on levels they couldn't handle alone. Again, Peter stepped in to pull the family together, trying to get everyone what they needed despite life being a complete asshole.

It'd been one tragedy after another, all set up like dominoes, and I'd had a terrible time dealing with it. Everything went zigzagged and over sideways, reaching such bloody scary depths and taking me with it like a black hole constantly sucking the joy out of life.

Dath had helped, talking me through the days when everything hurt too much to think beyond getting out of bed. He'd been there when the shitheap first hit, then for the bouts afterwards. I took as much compassionate leave as I could, nearly quit three times, and seriously considered hot-wiring the crap out of a ship every time I thought about going home.

Still, despite whatever happened planet-side, Peter and Mum told me to stay here. They refused to let me come back home, even if it never felt like it when I visited. Apparently, my best contribution to the whole mess was staying out here. If they hadn't tacked on "be happy, do important things, live your dream," I'd probably have agonized over what I'd done to be pushed away.

That hadn't stopped me from helping, though: chunks of my paycheques went to them, and Dath had helped me and Peter with finding financial assistance, medical care, and counseling, among other things.

Now I had Mack to turn to when the tough times reared up. We'd spent months bonding after Dath left, first over late-night snacks and discussion of what had happened with Dath, then over video games, where I'd shoot things to my heart's content and get myself into food hangovers from lollies, pizza, and beer that left Mack teasing me the next day. Somehow, that'd turned into dating, and we'd added watching natural disaster movies to our list of activities as we compared notes over dealing with aging parents. Loving Mack came so easily, with all that confident and cuddly *I've got this, babe* attitude xe had. I needed that, and adored Mack for wrapping me up in those warm, calming feels.

But Dath... I missed Dath. And as comforting as it was and wasn't, Mack missed him, too.

"Christ in a trash fire," I muttered, stealing one of Mack's expressions. The lift stopped on deck two, and off I went through the halls, pushing through three sets of doors before entering the mech bay proper. The place was like a gigantic warehouse, filled with tools and a variety of spacecraft under repairs instead of boxes of stuff. The bay smelled like a garage, the air thick with the taste of metal, paint, and oil, and the dark grey floor had scuff marks all over it. Racks of parts stood by the wall to my far right, while the rest of the bay was occupied by four ships, a seemingly haphazard mess of whatever was needed to fix them, and empty space where mechanics moved about and worked during the day.

There was someone here right now, the piercing high pitch of a drill making me wince. In a corner at the aft end of the bay sat a white research ship with *Sleipnir* painted on its side and front, accompanied by the Space Agency's logos and a Canadian flag. The outside of the craft was mucked up, dented and scraped, looking like it'd lost nearly every battle with the asteroid fields. As I approached, the inside didn't look any better, the frames of the open hatches charred like someone had set them on fire.

"What'd you do?" I shouted when the drill paused. "Roast chestnuts?"

Creaks sounded from inside the ship as Mack leaned out of the hatch on the starboard side, protective glasses on, hair tied back, and grease on xir blue t-shirt and cargos. "S'mores, babe. Always s'mores." Mack grinned and gestured to me with the drill in xir gloved hand. "We'll make a camper out of you one day, *meu chuchu*."

"Or not."

"Or maybe?" Mack waggled xir eyebrows and disappeared into the ship. A clatter later and Mack was back, walking towards me, the drill and glasses left behind as xe pulled off xir gloves and stuffed them into the back pocket of xir pants. Mack slipped a hand over the strip of xir dark hair, flattening down the frizz as xe grimaced. "Shit, dinner. I forgot."

"It's okay, babe," I said, leaning up for a quick kiss. Should I tell Mack xe tasted like xe'd been tonguing the wires? I pointed at the ship. "How's the patient?"

"*Fucked,*" Mack breathed, glancing back. "I've been working on the internals in my spare time, but there's a shitload of stuff to do. It really will take weeks to fix, even if we got all the parts tomorrow." Mack turned back to me with painful grimace. "It sucks, 'cause he's Dath's baby."

Yeah, I knew. I'd recognized the name of the ship and was trying hard not to think about it. I'd cry if George looked anything like this. I'd spent many a long hour designing and making that little guy, and I absolutely cherished him, right down to the pins of his finicky microcontroller.

"Hey." Mack brushed my cheek with the back of xir finger. "You okay?"

I shrugged, ignoring the gnawing in my stomach. "Knackered. Hungry."

Mack watched me, brown eyes narrowed for a second. "Worried and three days away from an ulcer?" Sighing, xe drew me in for a hug—one of our favourite pastimes, it seemed. Our default touch, at least, and one I cherished.

When I returned the hold, Mack squeezed tighter, no words needed to tell me what xe wanted to say. We just clicked that way and had since the day we finally sat down and got to know each other. Before that, I'd noticed Mack as we passed each other in the station or when I'd see xem with Dath, but nothing had happened between us. There had been times a simple glance from Mack had sent a bolt of interest through me, the thought of *What if xe weren't with Dath?* creeping into my thoughts on occasion, but that's all it'd ever been.

Once Dath had left, though, the barriers that kept us from talking finally collapsed. Instead of tearing each other down, we'd built each other up, finding common ground. Friendship came in the blink of an eye, woven between us through laughter and reminiscence, our heart-to-heart talks surprisingly fluid. Should it have been harder to get along with another ex? Maybe. I didn't know.

What I *did* know was that we went straight into full-on seeing each other without any of the casual we'd had with Dath. Mack and I were in partner-girlfriend mode, feeling right at home and comfortable—enough to talk about anything, including the deep-down feeling that we were missing one thing. One single element that was being entirely too bloody stubborn for anyone's good.

"Have you heard from Dath yet?" I murmured against Mack's chest, breathing in the grease and lingering scent of apple pie aftershave. Kind of gross in theory, but soothingly familiar.

"No," Mack said quietly, kissing the top of my head. "But you know he can take a while to respond to things." Xe gave me a lopsided smile. "Besides, these last few years could've really screwed with him. Give him a bit more time, yeah?"

"And maybe some encouragement," I added.

"Understanding."

"Suggestion."

"Hope." Mack played with the bobby pins keeping my bangs back, working them into place as xe gave me a sad little smile. "Security, because giving up everything takes everything else out of you. Sometimes you have to reach so far to regain so little."

"How about we try 'promise', then?" I nudged Mack's chin with my nose before I kissed xem, long and deep, sucking in the metallic taste on Mack's lips and the fading hint of lemon fizzy drink from xir tongue. "We tried once and got his attention. Phase two could give him a little more of that hope—if we make it clear enough. Assuming it's ready?"

Mack's grin could've given the Cheshire Cat a run for every dollar earned, xir eyes gleaming. "Oh, yeah, it's done. Sitting in my quarters right now, actually, ready to go. You just give me the count. T minus…?"

"Three days," I said, because anything could happen in three days. After all, Dath always said

three was a magical number.
I just hoped he saw the magic in us.

CHAPTER SIX
Sexy Trees and Freshly Frozen Hell

Dath
Friday, January 16th

Okay, *yes*, I was hiding from people. Mostly Kytzia and Mack, but also pretty much anyone else I could hide from. I needed people to go away. I needed work to disappear.

Or maybe I just wanted to crawl into bed permanently and pull a certain two somebodies in with me, then hide from the universe, because that sounded like paradise.

Complicated. My feelings were set on Fucking Complicated, while my body was set to Shitastic and quickly moving onto Freshly Frozen Hell. Other than feeling swamped by a To Do list that thought getting shorter was just a *suggestion*, I was overwhelmed with being here. Emotionally wrung out. There'd been a lot more to handle than I realized, even after adjusting my expectations within those first few days. Coming back, getting used to being here around *everyone*, both old and new colleagues, and then the shuttle wreck that was waiting to happen with Mack and Kytzia and whatever they had in their heads… I already knew I wanted to be part of that as much as I wanted to get out of here, but could I really go there with them?

Complicated. Confusing. Complex. Cornucopias of Confuciusly screwed cauli… Wait, now I was just making shit up.

I needed a right good smack. Hell, I'd settle for some actual sleep.

Tilting my head back with a defeated sigh, I settled back on the exercise bike and stared at the ceiling of the gym, legs still going at a constant, moderate pace as I rested my hands on my thighs. I'd already done my stint on the other machines in the room, mostly the leg press and chest press, with a bit of the rowing machine to really give my arms, legs, and back a workout. This was my cool-down; my transition back into remembering I had to leave and resume other life.

Life, which I'd been slugging through for a while now. It'd been a week since the visit from George, who I'd returned to Kytzia's office a couple days back when she was in a meeting with her higher ups. Since then, things were on a downward slope health-wise. I'd lain off the caffeine and continued nearly jabbing my eyes out to keep wearing the contacts, particularly with my usually decent far-sightedness in question as of late, but slowly—surely—new problems crept in. Other than feeling weaker than when I'd gotten back despite this exercise regime Doctor Cheche had prescribed, my sleep was shit. Fewer hours, fitful, and not entirely restful. It was budding insomnia, I could feel it, though I'd be happy if it stayed well away from Non-24, which had always made things unpredictable for Callie, even more so than the flavour of Delayed Sleep Phase Syndrome my dad dealt with. Though if whatever was going on kept spiraling down, it was something I couldn't afford to deal with. Something I didn't *want* to deal with, especially while I was at home. I wanted to enjoy every moment I was there, not view the world through the crappy lens of sleep deprivation.

I needed to touch down and connect with lake, land, and sky, which I could technically do now, considering how fast a ship would get me to Earth. Except I knew if I went back now, I wouldn't finish what needed doing before vacation began.

Adulting. Whose idea, again?

I glanced around the gym, my gaze mostly skimming the mirrors and machines. There were at least two dozen people in here with me, all of us getting our evening workouts in before Friday night really began. I'd opted to listen to the dance music playing on the speakers above, though several of the others had their own audio poison, their earphones sunk in deep. Or visual interests, as it was with the woman to my left, her attention on the tablet she'd perched on the bike handlebars with a documentary playing.

As the clock struck 2100, I wound down and dropped off the pedals, snatched my damp towel from the handlebars, and headed for my quarters. After two hours, I'd pissed off my growing aches and soft, squishy emotions the best I could. I'd earned the chance to get out of my sweaty track pants and t-shirt and take a shower.

Then maybe I'd see about that sleep thing. Going to bed early sounded like a good plan—after I lit a candle on my altar and asked the divine Caer Ibormeith to give me a right good push towards dreamland. I was sure I could sketch a pair of fair-looking swans in offering, maybe even pour Her a glass of the maple mead I kept in my room. Though if She was willing to listen, maybe I could get her husband's ear, too, because the gods knew I could also use help in the romance department. A little nudge from Aengus wouldn't be so bad, right?

I snorted as I rested my towel over my shoulder and stepped into the lift, then cleared my throat when I realized someone else was already there, talking on their phone. They got off on the deck before mine, leaving me in the soothing quiet for all of four seconds.

The rest of the journey back to my room was just as mundane, leaving me to wonder if I shouldn't go the extra distance on the spiritual side. Maybe I should level up and ask for help from Cernunnos and Cerridwen, two of the heavy hitters in my personal pantheon. Along with Danu, Brigit, the Dagda, and the Mórrígan, They were deities I'd turned to over and over since making a connection with the Celtic gods as a teen. Nature and knowledge, among the other things they influenced... How could I go wrong?

Though for good measure, maybe I'd also knock on the door to my family's pantheon, see if Frigga and any of her handmaidens pointed me in the right direction to resolve some of my troubles. Freyja, too, and possibly even Odin, though He was a long shot. We'd never really gelled, the All-Father and me. He preferred hanging out with my father, granting him all sorts of lovely moments as a dedicated Heathen. Odin also loved to play with Callie like Freyja did, though I suspected that was because of the seidr magic thing, considering Callie's admirable skills with shamanism and a talent for witchcraft. Between her and our mom, I still couldn't figure out who was the better kitchen witch... Not that there was a contest between them. Ever. *Cough, cough.*

Mulling over my choices, I stepped into my quarters, turned on the lights, and—

There was a tree.

In my room.

A freaking *tree* in my *room*.

More specifically, it was in the middle of the floor between me and the window, just sitting there, completely obvious.

So many questions, none of them fully-formed, though all of them ended in, *"the fresh fucking hell?!"*

The door slid closed behind me, making me jump. My attention went back to the tree, everything else forgotten as I moved closer. The top of the tree reached my knees, and it wasn't very large around—I could hug it if I dared. It resembled a white spruce or balsam fir in shape, but its leaves were all wrong: while it had several limbs of synthetic green needles, it also had flat, greenish-silver leaves that looked like an American elm's. I drew a finger over one silver leaf near the top, surprised by its cool metal as needles brushed the back of my hand.

The scribbles on the leaf surprised me more.

Frowning, I leaned down and tugged gently, trying to decipher the writing, until the leaf snapped out of its socket. Just a quiet snap, really, as though it was supposed to be removed instead of me outright breaking it. Confused more than worried, I read the small words etched into the metal, the leaf only about four inches long and nearly three inches wide.

I was certain my face flushed fire-engine red, because *fuck*.

"Tip to tip, slit to slit, come-drizzled everything

as I make you scream my name. Scream it, baby. Make it hurt."

I read the message again, stopping every few words. My skin burned, right to the tips of my ears. I tugged another leaf free. It too had writing:

"See how wet I can get, I dare you. Triple dare if it'll get you to fuck our brains out... Both of us at the same time."

That one made me choke as I bit my tongue, which really didn't help, considering the next leaf I pulled suggested someone biting a hell of a lot more of me than that.

I fell to my knees, half desperate to see if the other leaves said something, and half because standing was overrated when the rest of me was mortified to be hit on by what could've been the dirtiest tree I'd ever met.

And oh, how it *was.*

Every metal leaf I pulled offered another suggestion, almost all of them sexual, though the leaves close to the bottom were less explicit, if not mildly disturbing in a charming way:

"Hold me, love me, squeeze me, Cuddle Bunny. Let me nibble on your ear. Your neck. The cockles of your heart."

"Let's try a little role play: you be the gardener and I'll be the hole, deep and moist and ready."

"Come over, come under, let me ride you into the morning. Be my liquid fire, starshine."

The leaves closer to the top, however, they

were all porn-star-worthy:

"Finger fucked. Dick fucked. Tongue fucked. Any fucks you want to give, I'll spread for that."

"Rub it deep, cum bitter on my tongue. Nip your tip? No, I'll swallow it whole… and I don't spit."

Hot.

Damn.

I leaned against the bed, back pressed to the mattress and frame, a handful of leaves in my hand and my hard-on unhappy to be stuck inside my pants. It knew full well who'd set this up, and those two… Shit, they got A+++ for the effort, because yeah, my dick was awake and ready to surrender to whatever they wanted. Or maybe they should get an X+++ for making me forget about everything but them and the thought of the three of us sharing the same bed… the same kisses… the same everything.

Breathing deep, needing to cool the burn still tingling through me, I stared at the tree and the voids where once there had been silver leaves— twelve in all. It was one hell of a sexy Yule tree, erotic and dirty and crafty in ways I'd never have thought of, even if I factored in the *demi* part of my sexuality. Kytzia and Mack: they were speaking to me through a language I knew, one I loved deeper and harder the longer I sat there clutching the metal leaves. Combining botany with Brigit, goddess of smithing and crafting—not to mention inspiration and healing—they reached further through the distance I'd put between us, trying to pull me in. To pull me back. To re-forge what was broken.

I tossed down the leaves, save for the single leaf that had been at the very tip of the apex of the tree. That one had a different message than the others:

"Come to us. No joke. Let's talk. <3 K & M"

I groaned, the back of my head hitting my mattress, because I wanted. I *wanted.*

Fuck my life.

They'd gone to wowfully absurd lengths to get my attention, but I wasn't worth it. They knew which buttons to press, but making it work… Was I even together enough to go there with them? Or had I left too much of me in a far-off place, floating among the cold emptiness?

I could sleep it off for now. Cold shower it away. Think it to the depths of gone, tuning into isosceles triangles, spores, toe fungus—*anything* to get my mind off this. Because my head? It was killing me. My eyes burned. Everything was starting to ache and not in a good way, sharp pains jabbing and stabbing and dueling from one angle to another. Didn't matter how much I wanted them, I couldn't crawl my way over to them, not like this. Anything was sexier than the mess I was right now.

Save them from seeing this, that's what I'd do. With a whimper, I climbed onto my bed, leaves and sweaty towel discarded on the floor. I face-planted into my pillow, unable to stop grumbling at myself. This was the saddest shit going, and I'd been through my fair share.

A turn of my head brought the photo of Kytzia, Mack, and I into sight, the frame propped up on my nightstand. My heart sank deep enough that I wanted to throw it right up. So pretty, the two of them together. Could the three of us make it a beautiful triad? They seemed sold on the idea that we could. Could they be right? Was I dragging my heels for nothing, trying to out-stubborn them when I should've known better?

I grabbed the frame and drew it close, partially lying on top of it. I'd hold them like this for now, until it stopped hurting. Until the darkness that took me under finally let me go.

CHAPTER SEVEN
Hauntings of the Espresso Macaroon

Mack

Fifty bucks the tree's a failure.

That's what I had on my mind as I lay in bed, tossing and turning as usual, Kytzia snoozing to my right several inches away with her back to me. The alarm clock I was trying to ignore was to my left, on my bedside table, though I already knew it was close to 0300 hours.

I'd snuck the tree into Dath's quarters while he was at the gym after work, hoping he'd get the message and spend the rest of Friday night with us, not that we'd been doing much else but gaming.

Best laid plans and all.

Still no Dath, and no answer whatsoever. Both were even more disappointing now than after Kytzia's first try at getting him to come over, because we'd had fun with this one, thinking it was brilliant in an evil sort of way. But I understood. What we wanted was a lot to ask, especially since Dath had been away for *years*, not weeks or months.

Maybe he'd simply lost interest in us. It was a very real possibility we'd have to accept. It was also possible he was interested in someone else or not interested in anyone at all. Maybe that was the real reason he'd dumped us in the first place: maybe Kytzia and I had read him wrong. Maybe we'd wanted to see more in his words while he'd been telling us he wasn't into us anymore. I thought he'd liked what we had going—that closeness we'd found and the way we'd just clicked as friends, giving us the security of having someone to turn to no matter how far away from home we were. Maybe he was too scared to say he hated what we'd made our relationships with him—or he was pissed. I couldn't tell, not with him refusing to talk to either of us.

Sigh.

Perhaps it was time to back off for a bit, at least from the angle we'd been approaching him. We wanted an upgraded version of what we used to have, but we needed to strip everything down and focus on the core. Dath and I had been friends before we were lovers, no different than Kytzia and him, and that's where we needed to start. If nothing else, maybe he'd accept offers of friendship.

Turning onto my side, I watched Kytzia sleep. She snored ever so softly, which always made me laugh a little inside, because she was like a cat, getting into ridiculous positions and snoring with the quietest noises. It was cute as hell, and she didn't have any idea. It was my little secret, one I loved holding close and witnessing, just her and her adorable nose, stellar eyes, and pursed lips. I also loved when she made little duck faces while she dreamed. They always made me wonder what was going on in her head while she slept. I didn't doubt it was as brilliant as she was during the day—or more than fifty shades of fucking hilarious.

Christ, I loved her, and if she wanted Dath back, I'd do what I could to make it happen. For her. For us.

Frustrated by the sleep I wasn't getting, I pulled myself out of bed and slipped into a pair of purple PJ bottoms with anime princesses printed all over them, a white t-shirt, and a pair of black ballet flats, needing their lightness. As I resettled the blankets around Kytzia, letting her have the lot, I glanced over my room. It was nothing special: a standard set of quarters with a bed; a dresser that had a studded and spiked metal jewelry box on top, stuffed with my earrings and other shiny things; a couple of small, round tables by the window with chairs and boxes of junk metal; a desk with way more tech than I had room for; and a bathroom claimed by both my stuff and Kytzia's, including the hair and makeup products we traded back and forth.

It made me wonder, despite myself, what we'd *do* with a third person in our relationship, considering we'd have to get a bigger bed and make space for all those little items that somehow walked in without us really noticing…

Ugh, that didn't help my sleeplessness.

I padded out of my quarters and into the hallway, blinking at the brightness of the white light, even with it at half capacity. A wander could clear my head, at least enough for me to go back to bed and aim for sleeping in.

Yawning as I strolled through the forward section of deck eighteen, headed for port side, I couldn't help but think of what we'd been trying to get back to, Kytzia and I. We both had our specific loves for Dath. Both of us harboured a particular brand of gratitude for his existence during times when we struggled with not being physically able to be both here and on Earth at the exact same time, in the exact same moment.

The accumulation of everything I'd gone through out here and on the ground had led to me wanting something permanent and committed, I understood that now. It was that feeling of clicking so hard, so deep, with someone that I couldn't bear the thought of losing him, so I did what I could to pull him that much closer, praying nothing would come between us, *ever*. And out here, everything was put into entirely new perspectives, even if we could get home as fast as warp drive let us. Out here, the darkness gave us way too much time to think.

Dath and Kytzia both knew that raw, human side of me, almost right down to the smallest kernel of vulnerability in my soft, gooey middle. They'd both seen me lose my shit over things I'd wanted to get under control, because I hated feeling like life was spinning out and taking me with it. That was especially true when it came to *família,* and most definitely my kids, because like hell would I let life take me down when I had to be there for them. They'd already been through enough. The twins were twenty-two now, but that didn't erase a damn thing where their childhood was concerned.

I adopted my little *gêmeos* when they were four, after their mother, Isabella—my younger sister—died. Before that, I'd taken care of them when Isabella was too sick to do anything but struggle through her illness, unable to cope as a single parent. Once she passed, I took Siobhan and Tiago in permanently. My mam and *pai* helped with taking care of them, especially since I'd been working on my master's degree at the time, though I also had plenty of assistance from Miguel and Lula, my little brother and baby sister.

When Siobh and Ti were sixteen, wrapped up in teenage shenanigans and high school drama, that's when I was stationed at Crosspoint. Until then, I'd spent most of my time at the ground station with a few trips to Crosspoint, simply because I didn't want to get stuck out here by some freak accident when adolescence was doing its best to wreak havoc on our household. Not to mention that one of the stipulations of working at the space station was the permanent residence part, considering one of the weightier points of the Crosspoint program was to test the station to ensure it was durable and inhabitable for the long term. We weren't supposed to go back and forth to Earth on a regular basis, especially when travel used up resources and money that were needed elsewhere. Crosspoint was being tested to be a *home*, though I'd argued I already had one of those, and it was a good one. Yet ECHO kept trying to convince me to come out here, sweetening the pot with promotion after promotion until they were practically begging me to take over as manager.

Despite my doubts, I'd taken the job. Honestly, it was the best chance I had to really pull things together for Siobh and Ti. I knew we'd be slammed with post-secondary within a couple years, and I'd wanted them to have money for everything they needed, whatever they chose. Since then, I'd bounced between here and there when I could, making sure I was present for every holiday and during parts of their summer vacations. We vidchatted constantly. They pinged me until I wanted to kill every single ringtone and chime on my phone. I loved those little monsters, and I was happy to know they were both in a good place as people, both of them halfway through their fourth years at university.

Things hadn't always been so good, though, and that's where Dath had seen me at several of my weaker moments. Months before Dath left for Alpha Centauri, I'd been freaking out about Siobh and Ti going to university, on top of other stuff our *família* was going through. I was dealing with parents who'd finally decided to retire at a time when my *pai's* health wasn't so good. I was caught in the middle of being a kid while dealing with my own kids, all of my concerns and fears and questions thrown up into the air and raining down on me with a whole lot of *Ha, ha, fuck you* instead of solid solutions.

And sure, I was stuck on parent-mode, staring at the thought of an empty nest and wondering where that left me after giving Siobh and Ti more than fourteen years of myself. I'd worried about them moving on, each of them on their own and at different universities separated by thousands of kilometres. Panic attacks? Yeah, I'd had a few, right along with freaking out with them over the chances of them getting into the exact programs and schools they'd wanted: Marine Biology at UBC for Ti and Planetary Science at Western U for Siobh. Who'd known they'd actually *want* to be four provinces apart?

Thankfully, Dath had been here. He'd found ways to calm me down and reset my thoughts. He helped me take care of a few of the finer details. But mostly he was moral support, someone I knew I could unload on and he'd get it. He'd still been here come morning, giving me those sweet *You've got me, always* smiles and reminding me things weren't ever unsolvable, just challenging.

It was everything I'd missed, that gentle understanding and patience in his knowing grins. I'd needed them these last few years, especially whenever I was convinced that being manager was another way to shoot myself in the foot.

Flipping my tangled, untied hair back over my shoulder, I sighed at the lift as it settled and opened. I stepped in and thumbed the keypad for the observation deck. I was tired of narrow halls. I needed a bigger view of the world.

Be careful what you wish for, even if you never utter a word.

The lift opened and the first thing I saw was Dath, sitting on a bench beside the window directly across the way in dark sweatpants and a hoodie, one leg up, his elbow on his raised knee. He stared out the glass towards Earth, the obs deck quiet and almost completely dark around him. He looked lost, like he wondered why he was still here.

Me? I was glued to the lift until he glanced

my way, comforted by the soft, goofy smile he offered.

"Mind having some company?" I asked, then dared to step out of the lift to join him, casual but cautious. *Don't say no, not again—*

"Sure." Dath shifted to make space, both sneakered feet now on the ground. He gave me a glance-over as I sank down beside him. "Couldn't sleep, huh?"

I shrugged, still playing it cool even though part of me wanted to drag him back to my quarters and ruffle up that plum-coloured hair of his. "Happens. Though you're here, too, so you know how it is."

Dath snorted a laugh. "Considering I took a five-hour nap I hadn't planned on after everything else, yeah, I know it pretty well."

"Five-hour nap instead of coming by and fighting comic book rejects with us? I mean, *really*." I quirked my brow, trying to playfully feign insult, but the real thing seeped in between the words and punched me in the gut.

It seemed a bit of the tone carried over into serious for Dath, too: he dropped his gaze and twisted his fingers together in his lap.

"Not my first choice," he said softly, "just the one I needed to make. It was either that or pass out on your doorstep." His lips twisted in a sad, lopsided smile. "Not really how I wanted to make a comeback. Certainly not after the gift you left me. Figured you deserved better than that."

Huh. Okay. That sounded like progress, right?

"So… you got it then?" I asked, something clogged in my throat.

Seriously, self?! What the fuck was that, other than *duhhh*?

Kicking myself mentally, I let my head fall back and rolled my eyes. "And by 'got it,'" I added quickly, "I mean you didn't mind? I know down and dirty isn't your style, but we just thought…" I cleared my throat, whatever it was lumped there. "We took a chance, hoping you might still feel… want… that from us. Or anything, really," I mumbled.

Dath rested his hand between us on the bench, his arm briefly brushing my thigh. "I didn't mind, Mack," he said, so gentle and genuine I wished he'd say it again. "As for feeling…" He took a deep breath and let it out slowly. "That hasn't changed, even with what I said before, because what I said—it was bullshit, all of it. I didn't mean a word. I was too afraid to choose—to commit to losing either one of you. I didn't want to make the wrong choice and screw you or Kytzia over, so I freaked out and went for door three, which screwed us all equally… because *that* shit makes sense," he muttered. "My head wasn't in a good place, and I should've told you that. I should've talked to you—asked for your help, not run away."

A dozen questions snagged on my tongue, roadblocks where there should've been words. Well, damn. I'd been right the first time. But damn. Just… *damn*.

Dath glanced out the window. "And I'm sorry about it, I really am, 'cause it was such a shitty thing to do." He sighed, his head dropping a little as he faced me again. "I don't know how to make it up to you, or how I can say sorry enough, or what the hell to do now. I can't even come up with an apology that doesn't sound like shit. Four years," he said, laughing bitterly, "and all I can come up with is I'm sorry for hurting you and her, and I'm sorry I was the worst boyfriend ever. *Not* an award-winning apology."

"But an apology, nonetheless," I said, covering his hand on the bench with mine. "As long as you mean it, that's what matters. Dressing it up does dick all if the honesty isn't there."

We sat there in the silence, both of us staring at our hands.

After a while, Dath turned his palm into mine and grasped my hand with a light squeeze. "Can I ask you something?" A smirk tugged at his lips. "How are the half-pints? This new hairdo isn't because you ended up pulling it out over them, right?"

I laughed, maybe a little too loudly, though I didn't care. I was too preoccupied with loving the feel of his hand in mine. "No, this is a hundred percent shaved. And they're good. Ti's planning on Dalhousie for his master's. Siobh's committed to all sorts of things in London, so she's staying there for post-grad." I flashed him a grin and laced our fingers together. "She's got her eye on Crosspoint. Apparently, I need a chaperone."

Dath chuckled, leaning forward but never letting go of me. "I think it's payback for all those times you've shouted her name in public, making people think she should be shanking someone with an actual shiv."

"Hey, I wasn't the one who came up with the pronunciation, and the last time I called her by her first name, she told me off."

Another laugh from Dath. "She was *eight*, or so you said the last time you told me that story."

I grinned, a proud smartass. "Yeah, well, never argue with an eight-year-old. Or Kytzia, for that matter."

Dath sobered quickly. "How is she? Kytzia, I mean. She okay?"

Squeezing his fingers, I took a chance and pulled his hand into my lap. "She's got her days, but she's doing all right. Misses you." I caressed his thumb as I shifted closer until our hips touched. "We're doing good—her, me, everything that was going on before you left. It's been dealt with. Now we're just living."

"Moving on," Dath muttered.

"Matter of opinion," I countered. "Moving forward, but not away." I let out a ragged breath and slid my free hand over the skin bared on the right side of my head. "You fuck with our minds, you know that? Even when you're not here, you're *here*. Christ, it's been a forever of years, so seeing you again…"

At first Dath said nothing, just sat there nodding, but eventually he leaned into me, his chin on my shoulder. "And you aren't yelling at me because…?"

"Neither of us believed a word you said, even then," I answered quietly, shivering at how close we were. "It didn't add up, and we're pretty good at math, even the emotional variety. We wanted to call you out on said bullshit."

"So you punished me with a robot and a tree?"

I turned my head, bringing our lips close. His breath warmed my jaw, the fresh scent of coconut soap capturing my attention. "Why not? She really wanted to show you George, and the tree—" I teased his nose with mine. "You missed Christmas, asshole, so merry fucking New Year."

Dath snorted and laughed, his cheek pressed to my shoulder. "Guess I'll consider myself properly scolded."

"Hell, yes. Putting that tree together was a battle on its own." Okay, I lied. I hadn't even made it from scratch: we'd kept the tree in

Kytzia's quarters for the holidays, decorated and everything. For this purpose, though, I'd grabbed some junked metal and cut the leaves, then engraved them and jammed them into the core, replacing a few limbs of needles. But he didn't need to know that yet.

"Best tree in the space forest," Dath murmured, our lips close once again.

The ghost of a kiss haunted us both, a hint of touch that was more breath than skin. Merely the silence reaching out, words pushed aside, waiting for someone to put their mouth where their meaning was.

That kiss came crashing down like a boulder through a glass barrier, hard and full of intent, enough to make lips bleed and jaws burn. I didn't know who started it, and I didn't care, just kissed back, feeding off everything he gave. Fuck, it was like it used to be. Still so good. He smelled like coconuts and tasted like coffee, all sweet and bitter like an espresso macaroon. I'd gnaw at his lips all night if he'd let me.

A hand slid across my waist and tugged me closer. His fingers slid up the back of my neck. Hell, yes, I missed this. The needy kisses we could draw out for hours; the tender touch that said *Screw you, world, we're busy*. If he wanted them back, I was all in. Me and my hands that were busy drawing him as close as we could get, practically pulling him into my lap, nowhere near concerned that my arousal was painfully obvious and wanted more than I did that night.

"Come back with me," I said against his lips before going in for another kiss, this time softer as I cupped his cheek. "Let's start over, tonight. Now."

"She won't mind?" Dath took a breath that I stole just as quickly, nipping at his lips.

"She's been waiting for days. Trust me, she'd rather wake up to find you there than not."

That seemed to settle him. The next moment, I was up and leading him from the observation deck to my quarters, hand in hand until we were in my room. I shucked my flats and shirt as Dath tossed his hoodie and sneakers aside, drawing my focus to all the lovely naked skin on display. I slipped into the bed on Kytzia's left while Dath nudged her shoulder a bit.

Kytzia moaned, turned over, then startled awake. She glanced at me first, confusion accompanying every blink, strands of dark red and light blue hair falling across part of her face. "What's going—?" Her gaze snapped back over her shoulder as she twisted towards Dath. "Hey, you…"

"Mind if I join the slumber party?" he asked.

Kytzia wasted no time: she shuffled closer to me, allowing him to slip under the covers. "Happy birthday to me," she breathed once he settled, reaching back to caress his cheek.

Dath smirked and kissed her fingers. "It's not even your birthday, not-birthday girl."

"No," I argued, planting a kiss on Kytzia's bare shoulder. "Today it *is*. And tomorrow, and the day after…"

"For however long I get this," she said with finality, casting a glance to me, then Dath.

Neither of us said a word, just smiled at her, at each other, and snuggled down around her. Whatever tomorrow brought didn't particularly matter. For tonight, we were here, finally together, content to drift into sleep without worries or the need to apologize for past mistakes. Like the rest of the universe, all of that could wait. We needed this more.

CHAPTER EIGHT
What's A Little Sacrifice, Anyway?

Dath
Friday, January 23rd

My body may have been falling apart bit by bit, but my heart was lighter than it had been in years.

Humming along to the electro-pop music coming from Vena's office two doors down from mine, I plugged away at the parameters of the last set of analyses I wanted to run on the plants from Alpha Centauri. I'd prep them now then let Farah and Zsuzsi take care of things while I was on Earth. There were a million things to learn about these species: biochemistry, behaviour, microbiology, genetic sequences, their relationships to their environments and each other—the entire lot, all of which took time. I was just thankful I had a team that knew what they were doing.

The rest of my stress was slowly thinning out like a crawling fog. I felt like absolute crap, but my To Do list had a big dent in it, so huzzah to small victories. There still wasn't any good news on the ship repair front, though bless Mack for trying to soften the blow for me with the warmth of dark humour and heartfelt hugs. Hell, I was just happy to have *Mack* back, fuck the ship.

Mm, Mack and Kytzia.

I smiled lazily in recollection and tapped the keys on my laptop in rhythm to the music, one phrase away from singing along. It'd been a week since I'd taken that second chance Mack and Kytzia had offered, and there wasn't any going back. They were that bit of wonderful that made this place actually start to *feel* like a home.

My heart did a funny little flip and flutter, completely in agreement. Which was great, because my head was being an ass again as the pain meds wore off and revived the dull ache I'd gotten used to. I was still having trouble sleeping, though it wasn't so bad when I cuddled up close to Mack and Kytzia—at least when we dared to sleep in the same bed, cramped and finding every awkward position known to a triad. That was a matter Mack intended to fix, though, and soon.

I simply rolled along with it all, taking nothing for granted. When Kytzia demanded I talk nerdy to her, I happily dug deep into geek-mode and pulled out some real gems that had her laughing even hours later. I'd do anything she wanted if it kept her laughing and smiling like she'd sic George's evil bastard of a twin on anyone who tried to break us up.

And Mack… I'd follow Mack anywhere. I'd felt that way almost since the beginning, our friendship coming so easily. Love had dozens of faces and countless layers, and they showed so clearly with Mack. Leaving that behind had torn me apart more than I'd realized, like I'd scraped away parts of myself and replaced them with cotton to soften the blows to come, all the while not realizing I'd also stripped away who I wanted to be.

Returning to Kytzia and Mack was more than a second chance at romance and relationship: it was an open door to reconnecting with myself and touching down on stable ground after being adrift in the chaos of shadow and doubt. Every moment I spent with them was the tiniest whisper of need, telling me I needed to stick with them—and I would, for as long as they'd put up with me.

Our plans tonight were no exception. I snuck a glance at the time on my laptop: almost noon. Damn, that still left seven hours until we met for dinner and took a go at a new virtual reality program Kytzia had found in the free-tech rec rooms—FTRs, we called them, where users could do whatever they wanted within the systems available, including exploration of virtual realities, simulations, and holograms. I had a feeling tonight's plans included something to do with superheroes, because Kytzia had messaged me earlier about my feelings on tights and capes, followed by a string of questionable emojis that included halos and devil horns.

Or maybe those were for much later in the night, wherever we ended up. We hadn't done full-on sex yet, only petting, though apparently a bit of oral was coming up next, except it wasn't scheduled for a specific time. What *did* appear to be planned, however, was the slow slide into intercourse and the rest of its friends. According to Kytzia and Mack, I'd been away for *far* too long, so slow was how we would do things until we all felt I was comfortable with them again.

Sweet as that was, I'd read their answer deeper than maybe they'd wanted me to: their choice of words spoke more to my demisexuality than discomfort from getting fucked by Mack or being ridden by Kytzia.

I'd been honest with them from the beginning: I was happy without sex, content to bypass it altogether in favour of the emotional connections that gripped me and held tighter than any physical desire. But with a rare few, individuals that I knew well and cared for deeply, those connections could veer into strange little corners and I'd find myself wanting the physical aspect, too.

What I had with Mack and Kytzia had gone there some time ago, tapping into the quieter part of me that wanted a taste of their bodies as well as their souls. Those feelings hadn't eroded these last four years. The bonds remained, drawing me to them in all ways, but it seemed they thought it all could have died and gone away. They treaded carefully, giving me all the space to say no, and I loved them for it, even if that wasn't how things worked with me.

A work in progress, that's what we were. Maybe slow *was* the way to go, just not for the exact reasons they thought. There was a lot to learn and relearn, especially when we'd never been three before, just two and two. In some ways, we were rewriting everything between us, not to erase the old but merely revise it to make us stronger. To bring us closer and fill in the blanks we hadn't been able to previously.

Either way, I was with them, however this went down. We'd already established our tone and harmonies; now we'd find our rhythm and pace. If that meant I could tongue the silver horseshoe barbells in Mack's nipples and finger Kytzia into biting her pillow just to show them *precisely* where my interests were at, then I was *there*.

For now, however, I needed to be elsewhere. The moment the clock struck 1200, I was up and out of my office, my personal tablet and a mug of feverfew tea in my hands as I returned to my quarters for my lunch hour. I had a call to make.

After grabbing the cloth-wrapped bundle of scrap metal rod and wires from my top dresser drawer, I laid the bundle on my desk with a pair of wire cutters and propped my tablet on its stand before hitting the "Call" button.

A ringtone later and my mom's face popped up on the screen, her greying brown-black hair styled in a pixie cut around her oval face, her brown eyes brightened by her smile. Her skin was olive like mine, and I resembled her more than any else, though my eyes were green like my dad's. "Hey, ho, kiddo! How goes it?" she greeted with a wave.

I waved back and sat down, setting down my tea. "It's goin'. You?"

"Ah, just a regular Friday," Mom answered, flicking her wrist towards the rest of the home office behind her, most of it bookshelves across the green walls. "I've got essays to grade and all that. Regular death-to-red-pens sort of stuff." She grinned, her scrunched nose adding to the wicked gleam in her eyes. "Here they thought a distance learning teacher was code for 'nice.'"

"Ha! Suckers," a second, higher voice added from her end. Callie stepped into frame behind Mom and cackled as she cuddled a kitten close, its black head under her chin. "What up, bro?" she asked. Her long, dark brown hair was half-down, the other half twisted and coiled up into small buns perched on top of either side of her head, rogue strands hanging loose. She had olive skin, too, though paler than mine, and her eyes were the same swampy green as mine behind her glasses with their bright green frames. While Mom wore a crisp white button-up shirt and charcoal-grey pinstripe vest, Callie was an image of winter, bundled up in an over-sized, cream-coloured knit sweater with gigantic pockets, a dark fuchsia turtleneck, and black jeans. A gold pentacle the size of a pickle jar lid hung around her neck on a black chain. "And before you ask, this—" Callie held up the kitten. "—is Silbhester. He's our newest baby."

He was a cute little ball of fluff, I'd give her that, all black on top with a white belly, feet, and half of his face. There was a black patch on his nose that would've been perfectly symmetrical if it weren't skewed to the right.

I nodded at Callie. "'Sup, sis. How many cats is that now?"

"Five, and shut up," she said, lips pursed. "You didn't say anything about *not* taking in rescues when we leased the house from you."

Hands up, I sat back. "Hey, wasn't gonna say a thing. You're a cat girl. I'm going to accept it and move on." I grinned and waggled my brows. "You know, until I get back and exact my revenge."

Callie flipped me the middle finger and stuck out her tongue.

Mom sighed. "Children. Let me know when you grow up, okay? Then I might finally write you into our will."

"Yes, Mom," we intoned together, rolling our eyes.

"So, what's happening since we talked last week, puddin'?" Mom leaned forward, her face coming in close. I spied the silver chain under her collar, her rainbow-coloured crystal pentacle and triple moon pendant tucked under her shirt. "You look better."

"Thanks," I muttered, unwrapping the bundle in front of me. I pulled out the narrow metal rod and pre-cut wires, all courtesy of Mack, who'd salvaged them from the mech bay's junk pile for me. The stainless-steel rod was about half a foot long, perfect for making a Brigit's Cross, and the mix of copper and aluminum wires were roughly the same length. Usually I made a Brigit's Cross on Imbolc with Mom and Callie, using straw, braided raffia, or reeds and rushes if we could get them, then I'd bring the cross back and place it on my altar. This year, however, I wanted one before the holiday. I needed the comfort, that calm that came from tradition and the connection to my spiritual roots, as well as needing to thank Goddess Brigit for a few particular blessings I'd been granted as of late. Had She gotten a kick out of that sexy tree like I had?

"And things are good—really good." I smiled as I held the rod vertically in my left hand and folded one of the copper wires perfectly in half around the rod, horizontal across the rod's middle with the ends of the copper wire in my right hand. "I'm seeing someone. Well, two someones," I corrected, turning the rod-wire frame counter-clockwise by ninety degrees. I repeated the folding motion with the next copper wire, this time over the first wire, which was in vertical position as the rod had been. "All three of us, together."

Callie whooped as I held the wires tight to the rod. I caught Mom's smile while I turned the weave ninety degrees counter-clockwise again.

"That's great news, sweetheart," Mom said, leaning back, all pleased as she winked at me. "See? Told you to keep your chin up. You never know what you'll find."

"Forgiveness," I mumbled, folding a third wire over both the second wire and the rod. I turned the cross again and added a fourth wire, keeping everything tight. I'd made so many of these over the years, I could do it with my eyes closed. I'd even made them from straws and zip ties—anything I had on hand that could be folded, really. It was a soothing motion, the routine of adding and turning, and sometimes I found myself absentmindedly making one like other people doodled.

That familiarity was how I could look at the screen and catch Mom's questioning expression. Aw, crap. I'd used my out-loud voice, hadn't I?

"*Reeeally*," Callie said, her brow quirked like Mom's, gaze full of questions.

"Yo, Callisto, *shoosh*." I glared at her. "Or I'm calling you Amalthea from here on out until forever." Yeah, Callisto Amalthea was her name, almost as fun as mine. Though honestly, she'd had better luck in the getting-named department: at least *hers* were after legit figures in Greek stories that'd also had their names given to moons and constellations. Yet *I* was the one in space. The joke wasn't lost on me.

"Aww, baby, we're just curious." Mom tilted her head. "Sounds like there's a story there."

"A long and fucked-up one." I continued weaving the cross, constantly adding a wire, pulling it tighter around the centre, then turning. "I'll tell it to you once I'm home. It's not really… Friday afternoon talk." I winced. It was more of a *lemme get drunk first* story.

"Uh huh." Callie snuggled with the kitten, who'd fallen asleep in her hands. "So you're still planning on being here next weekend, right?"

"Yup. We'll hang out all Saturday and Sunday afternoon, then we'll split ways for Imbolc, as usual." That had been our tradition since Callie and I were late teens: while the three of us celebrated the same eight holidays in the Wheel of the Year, we observed them through rituals—"rits" for short—with our own specific groups of people, or by ourselves. Mom and Callie celebrated them as Sabbats with their Wiccan coven, and I as festivals with my local Druid grove, keeping our traditions apart. Dad did neither, instead keeping to the Heathen traditions with his kindred, participating in every blót, sumble, and other gathering they had.

To say there was a lot of Pagan in our family was an understatement. Growing up, there'd always been *plenty* of gods and goddesses in our household, all meeting around our family altar without much fight. Then again, Mom and Dad constantly offered up high-quality mead and the *good* food to keep the peace, so maybe everyone was merely sated and jovial, I didn't know. All I knew was that we had a host of spiritual visitors pass through and leave their mark, and we'd found a way to make it work, yet we kept our individuality intact and didn't kill each other in the process. In our family, debate was healthy and everyone chose their own way, especially if we were the ones being chosen. Because shit, saying no to the likes of Thor, Hekate, or Bast when they came knocking? Around us, that was better known as *just don't do it*.

"But...?" Mom asked.

I stopped, staring at the cross instead of the screen as my face warmed with a blush. I hadn't realized there'd *been* a 'but' in my tone.

"*But* I was thinking... I might bring a couple guests... if they want," I answered, stilted and weird, my voice cracking in the middle. I cleared my throat and focused on tightening the wires. I didn't know if Mack and Kytzia were ready to meet the rest of the clan yet. And eat. A lot. And drink Mom's cider... a lot. And possibly freeze their toes off during the rit… maybe just a little. We'd chatted about the possibilities briefly, with both Mack and Kytzia saying they'd come celebrate with me if I wanted them around for some of my vacation. Mack was a lapsed Roman Catholic with pantheistic leanings, and Kytzia wasn't terribly against spirituality or religion, so the chances of them showing up if I asked really nicely… There was a *maybe* in there.

But crap, I also needed to talk to Gina, our grove's coordinator. I'd never brought anyone to one of our rits before. I needed to clear it with the group first. Eh, I'd do that tonight. I needed to get my lines for the rit, anyway, and what was I going to take for the potluck feast? I could cook something if I figured out a tasty dish, or I could slow cook the hell out of a stew, but I did not *bake*. Hockey pucks. I could make maple-drowned, oat-packed hockey pucks. That was as good as my skills got in the baking department. It still didn't solve the problem of *what* to take, however, and the time to put it together, especially if I didn't have much time between being bombarded by family, cats, and whoever else wanted to welcome me home.

Maybe I could bribe Callie or Samine, her wife, to make something. They used my kitchen anyway—

Fuck!

My head practically exploded—at least that's how it felt. The mid-thought *blam!* of pain blasted through my head, around my eyes and behind them, then pinged off everything in my skull like a pinball. Whimpering, I dropped the cross and grabbed my head.

"*Dath?*" Mom called. "Sweetie? You okay?"

"No..." I croaked out, wincing as the pain refused to subside. Gods, it felt like someone was trying to suck my eyeballs into a wine bottle while cracking open my skull with a can opener. The hell?!

"Baby, you don't look so good—"

"Dath!" Callie snapped her fingers. "Med bay, *now*. Go." Her image was blurry as she neared the camera. "And tissues, kid. Get a tissue. You're bleeding."

"What?" I squinted at the screen, my palm over my right eye. The pressure helped a little.

"Nose."

I swiped under my nostrils. My finger came away bloody.

Shit.

I hurried to the bathroom the best I could without tripping, my head hating the jiggling. I grabbed the box of tissues and shoved two under my nose. Keeping my head down, I returned to the desk. Yeah, med bay it was. Another dose of meds wasn't going to cut it. "Sorry, I need to—"

Mom waved me off. "Go! Get seen to. Call later, okay? Check in?"

"Yeah. Love you." With that, I ended the call,

pushed the unfinished Brigit's Cross aside, and hugged the tissues close on my way to the med bay.

<hr />

I was there within five minutes, then was poked and prodded fifteen minutes after that by two nurses and Doctor Cheche. Needle, needle, and, oh, look, *another* needle. Blood pressure: check. Pupils: still in my head. Breathing: yep, I wasn't a zombie, thank the gods. Lymph nodes: swollen. Fantastic.

"We'll run all the tests," Doctor Cheche assured me. They smiled, though it wasn't the happy kind. "I don't want you to be overly worried right now."

"But there's some concern, yeah?"

Doctor Cheche sighed and fell into a chair by the bed I sat on, all white coat, dark slacks, and a blouse that was a bright sky blue on their deep brown skin. They held their tablet close, their stethoscope clacking against the black casing. "Yes, there's some concern," they said, brushing their shoulder-length black hair over their shoulder, "but we want to keep your stress levels down. Get your blood pressure to a friendlier number." Doctor Cheche frowned. "As for this getting worse over time instead of better… Not such good news, though maybe it's your body having difficulty getting used to being back."

My skepticism must've made it into my glance, because Doctor Cheche sighed and shook their head a second later. "Any number of things can happen after you get back, Dath, especially since you were gone for years. If space habitation can modify how we express genes and change the bacteria in our guts, it can do *a lot* of other things to the body. You know that."

Yeah, I did, but it didn't make it *not* suck. Although my pain had leveled out since coming into the bay, it was more of a stuffed-in-a-can feeling now than the awful searing pain from earlier. I was grateful when one of the nurses gave me a stronger painkiller than I'd been using.

"For now, we'll run the tests, monitor your vitals," Doctor Cheche said. "I want you to keep a log of symptoms—changes, severity, and complications. Anything we can use." They smiled, their blue eyes softened with amusement. "You're used to collecting data, so it shouldn't be difficult for you. Just *please*, keep your stress under control until we get this resolved? Try to not push yourself too hard, keep up your exercises, and *don't* overdo anything."

Ha.

Sure.

Fuck my life.

CHAPTER NINE
No, Vacation Isn't Spelled
Q-U-A-R-A-N-T-I-N-E

Kytzia
Sunday, January 25th

"Quit playing with my feet!" I shrieked, game controller in my hand as I scrambled across the floor of my quarters away from Mack. On the big-screen TV on the bathroom side of the room, my wood elf died a horrible, gurgling death at the hands of ogres.

Mack only laughed, husky and deep, then prowled towards me on hands and knees, xir dangly, silver tassel earrings swaying with every move. Dath didn't even try to help: he just sat on the mussed-up purple sheets on my bed and chuckled his arse off, clutching his controller close and his cold compress closer.

Bloody lovers.

"Hey, big bad, lay off the wolfing," I told Mack, pointing a not-so-threatening finger at xem. Ugh, why was I still giggling? Stern. I needed to be stern. "Or I'll huff and puff right on back—and there won't be *any* blowing."

Mack stopped and sat back on xir legs, not at all convinced—not with that grin on xir face. "Mm, sure thing, little red. I'll just go play with my goods, butter up my breadstick, and put them *all* into someone else's basket." Xe threw a devilish look over to Dath, who stopped laughing long enough to realize what Mack had said. Another one of Dath's sweet blushes coloured his cheeks, and he sputtered as he sipped his tea—or tried to, what with all the dribbles running down his chin from cough-laughing

Our baby was such an adorable mess sometimes.

"Aw, come on. You're corrupting fairy tales for him, love." Up on my feet, I abandoned my controller on the floor and climbed onto the bed, the video game forgotten until Dath paused it. I took the tea from Dath and placed it on the floor before straddling his lap, his legs still crossed under me. I knew he'd been feeling crook these last couple days, and he looked a bit flush, all our play aside. We were spending the weekend together, all three of us, and we'd kept an eye on Dath, sneaking the occasional subtle check for fever and nausea.

For the moment, he seemed content, his arms coming about my waist, a soft smile on his face. "They were corrupted long before this, babe. You've never met my sister or her BFFs—or my parents, for that matter. Then again," Dath said, tossing Mack a *look*, eyes and lips showing his amusement, "there was also a certain Snow White one Hallowe'en a few years ago. Something about whips, chains, and cuffs on xir belt instead of a chatelaine or anything *remotely* innocent?"

Mack's wicked laugh played through me until I shivered. With my arms around Dath's neck, I held tight as Mack pushed off the floor and kneeled on the bed. "Never said I liked my fairy tales innocent," xe murmured, slowly kissing a path along Dath's cheek, down to his neck as Dath tilted his head to the side and gave Mack the space to play. "Besides, we had a great time at that party. One hell of a glitter vodka hangover the next morning, your vampire makeup all smudged. Loved that sexy, morning-after immortal look."

Now *that* was an image I'd replay a few hundred times. Even more if we could get Mack to dress to match. Xe was already wearing black eyeliner, black nail polish, and dark, moody clothes, so the rest…

"Really?" I grinned at Dath, then at Mack. Oh, was I *ever* banking these thoughts. Something to explore on Valentine's Day, perhaps? "Sounds like we have entirely too much catching up to do. I vote we work on that."

Before either of them answered, I laid a kiss smack dab on Dath's lips, nowhere near playing soft and sweet. His response was just as hard, intentions coming through loud and clear, so I kicked it up a notch, rolling with tongue and harsh nips and everything I had that could make an epic quest of his mouth on mine.

When we parted—just for a second, to get a breath—Dath's head tilted back, his lips suddenly occupied by Mack's. Mack, who was up on xir knees, one hand in Dath's hair and the other around his throat, pulling him close as they went at it. Dath's grip tightened around me, and I couldn't help but grind against him, see where his comfort levels were at. I could watch them all day. We could even make a bloody good piss up of this. It was only 1600 hours. Grab a case of ciders, turn on some mean tunes, and we could have a right good time sucking off each other's faces. Maybe even make Dath forget what the doctor—

"Wait." Dath pushed Mack away, his face flushed. "I need—I can't—" He moaned and grabbed his head with one hand. "Dizzy. Can't..." Whimpering, he leaned his forehead against mine.

Well, so much for making Dath forget.

"Baby?" I cupped his cheeks. He *did* feel a little warm. Only a little, though. "You okay?"

"My head," he answered, quiet as he took a slow breath and grimaced. "Fucked again."

Mack threw me a worried glance, never once letting up xir massage on the back of Dath's neck. Okay, piss up cancelled. I had another plan in mind.

"Baby, let's go down to the cafeteria, yeah? We'll get some air." I shared a nod with Mack. "Get you a fresh cuppa and some of that heal-all-your-ills chicken soup. It's Sunday anyway—we'll play it quiet as." Once I climbed out of Dath's lap, I pulled him up. He was unsteady on his feet, leaning into me until Mack pulled him against xem, one arm around Dath's back.

"'Kay," Dath said, smiling at me as he steadied.

Mack's arm stayed around Dath on our way out of my quarters, Dath's hand in mine. "Hey, only five more days until we get to go home and meet your family," I said, keeping our pace slow as we walked through the corridor. We weren't the only ones moving about: some passed us on their way to wherever, while others hung out in the hallway, chatting and laughing.

"Earlier, if I'm lucky," Dath muttered.

"Whenever you're ready," Mack said quietly. "*Sleipnir's* a write-off for now, but I've got another ship set to go. You just tell me when."

I hugged Dath around his stomach. "Me, too. I've already booked the time off, and Mack's xir own boss, so hey, whatever."

The shyest grin crept across Dath's face. "Thanks." He kissed the top of my head, then stole a kiss from Mack, all the while holding onto us both. I *knew* we could make this work—us, without the unnecessary crap in the way. So far, we'd fallen into being three rather easily, no drama. Maybe the trip back to Earth would help us cement this relationship further; give us a shared experience we could use to make up for lost time and bring us even closer, as if the last few years hadn't really happened. This was a second go at something we should've tried the first time around, and I didn't intend to let any of us squander it.

We rounded the corridor towards the lift, Dath at least able to walk without tripping, so there was that. He looked absolutely knackered, though, and winces—there were a few of those. I wished I could kiss that pain away, but the painkillers he'd been taking all weekend were the only kisses of relief that seemed to work. He'd even forgone both his glasses *and* his contacts, so his game characters had ended up dying more than succeeding at anything since he couldn't make out details that would've helped.

Still, he went through the motions with us, trying his best not to act like something was wrong. He wasn't the best bullshitter in the universe, but we'd let him have his moments. At least he wasn't pushing us away anymore. He trusted us to take care of him instead of turning away.

Twenty feet from the lift, the hairs on the back of my neck stood on end. Goosebumps rose on my arms.

Didn't know what tipped me off, but I felt the alarms before they sounded.

It was like a whisper of electricity zapped through me before blaring sirens filled the halls, the noise bouncing off my eardrums and killing my head. Lights above flashed red and blue, white light flickering in between. Doors sealed shut on either side of us. The lift stopped mid-journey, even as someone jabbed at the touchpad to call it to our deck. The lift and its doors would remain inaccessible until the alert was over or until someone overrode the system.

Crosspoint was on lockdown, and judging by the voice on the PA system, the med bay wasn't in the mood for playing around.

"*The fuck!*" Dath cried out, his hands clapped over his ears, eyes squeezed shut. Mack pulled him close, one arm wrapped around Dath's head.

"… Please remain in your area…" the PA system repeated. "This is a level three medical emergency. Full-station lockdown is in effect. Medical personnel have been dispatched and containment is underway. Please remain in your area…"

Behind us, the door to the stairwell opened, and a team of said medical personnel busted through with several security guards.

"*Bloody hell*," I muttered, covering my ears. The med bay people were dressed in white hazmat suits, and the security guards in black protective gear carried *very* visible tasers on their tact belts.

Lovely.

What wasn't so lovely was how they stared at Dath, then me and Mack, hands up in front of them in peaceful approach.

"We need you to come to the med bay, folks," one of the medical staff said—Doyle, I think? He moved closer, two guards at his side, everyone ready to grab and go. "There's been a… complication. We need to get you tested."

"For what?" I yelled over the alarm.

Guy-who-was-likely-Doyle glanced at Dath again, and I wanted to flick his face. "Just… Med bay. We need to handle this in the med bay."

"If it'll get you to stop this—" Dath started, but never finished. He doubled over, arms wrapped around his waist.

Next I knew, he tumbled over and hit the floor face-first.

"*Dath!*" I sank down, nearly crashing shoulders with Mack as we turned Dath over. He groaned, winced, fought to cover his eyes and ears, looking frustrated that he couldn't do both at once. *Dammit!* I wanted to hold him close and bash that shit away for him until he gave me the all-clear.

I leaned over but never got the chance to hold: someone pulled me back, up to my feet, then I was watching Dath get further and further away as I was dragged down the hall by my arm.

"Quit it!" I yelled, but it didn't matter. Medical staff descended on Dath like vultures, handling him, getting him to his feet. They may have thought they were being gentle, but like hell did it help. Mack was grabbed, too, and led away like me, but in the opposite direction. I couldn't answer Mack's raging *the fuck is this* glare with anything other than my own *I'll sic a death bot on them* glower.

"So much for keeping his stress down!" I shouted and yanked my arm back from the medical officer. I'd go to the med bay on my own, thanks, then I'd give them an earful about it. They could test whatever they wanted, but they'd better take care of Dath and Mack or I'd hack their arses so bad they wouldn't be able to escape any Screen of Death for at least three months.

Yeah, that's right. Scary shit was only scary until I got to my tech. If they 'complicated' this any more than they already had, there were a dozen chunks of code I could pull out to show them what complicated *really* looked like.

This had better be good.

———— •❧• ————

Monday, January 26th

Dath looked terrible, pale and fragile, worse

than when he'd first returned from Alpha C.

Okay, so maybe there'd been a valid point to his being dragged away to med bay, and *maybe* I'd overreacted… ish. More like got a little touchy… ish.

Either way, Mack and I were standing outside of the isolation unit and Dath wasn't. That wasn't okay. Our baby didn't even *look* like himself, wrapped up in a blue hospital gown with tubes and wires coming out and going in, doing whatever they were apparently supposed to do.

With a groan, I hugged Mack and continued watching Dath through the window into the isolation room, a unit they usually used for cases of contagious illness. Mack and I had been in med bay for the last twenty-five hours, subjected to tests and treatments for all but one of those hours. Whatever the doctors had thought we might have, we didn't seem to be carrying, so they'd let us go on a *Come here ASAP if you feel anything bad* pass.

Other than us, the med bay had been testing other station staff all day and night, in hopes they'd catch anyone else who could possibly be infected with whatever Dath had.

'*Whatever* Dath had,' because the doctors had no idea what it was. At least not down to a name or origin or a solid treatment. They knew he had *something* ickily alien—something he'd brought back from Alpha C—but they were still working on it, having discussions with the microbiologists and virologists on board. They'd also been in talks with Dath's mission crew, who they'd brought in at the same time as us with separate medical staff-security teams, though they didn't display any symptoms, either.

I didn't know everything they wanted to look at, but I *did* know they'd knocked Dath out for a few days and were running every test they could to understand what was making him sick. He was worse than they thought, and they had all manners of people coming in to give him a jab, none of which made the situation better. He'd be in quarantine until they were convinced he wasn't a threat any longer. Until then, no one else left the station, and those who'd already left were being tested at the ground station.

I didn't care about anyone else right now. Dath and Mack were my concerns. Mack, with xir arms around me, calm and protective despite the fact xe hated this as much as I did, and Dath, who was sedated for who knew how long.

"It'll be okay, *coração*," Mack whispered, smoothing down my hair. "They'll figure it out." Xe kissed my forehead. "For now, we'll think good thoughts. Positive energies."

I sighed and cuddled closer. Positive was difficult when we could be staring at Dath as he died slowly. All that time with us and we didn't even realize…

That hit me hardest, the fact we hadn't seen it

for what it was. Once more, life was ripping the rug out from under me without a pillow to land on. We should've noticed it was something terrible well before now.

Even worse? He'd been so excited to go home. His family was waiting to see him—family he hadn't hugged or been around for more than four years. He'd had plans, ones he'd wanted to share with us. We'd also wanted him to meet *our* families. Mack was dying to put Siobhan and Dath in the same room to see what sorts of hilarious things came out of it, and I wanted to see if Peter and Dath got on the way I expected they would.

Those plans were a bust. The holiday that meant so much to him would come and go before he got out of here. Hell, before he even *woke up*, at the rate the doctors were talking.

It wasn't fair, none of it, but what could we do? We were out here, he was in there, and the distance between us seemed so much further than when he'd been in Alpha C. I could steal a ship right now and be light years away from here in no time, but I couldn't get any closer to Dath than this bloody window. After years of waiting for him to come home, this was what we were left with.

Baby, where are your gods now? I asked silently, pressing my palm to the window. *Because they certainly aren't here.*

But we were. We'd always be here. I'd camp

out in this exact spot for however long it took. I'd stick George on the window with a camera to keep an eye out whenever my eyes closed. Then once Dath was cleared, we'd walk him out of here and right back to where he belonged: in our arms, away from the nastiness of the universe, because it couldn't have him. It'd had its chance out there in Alpha C, and it'd sent him home. He was ours now. He was family. If there was anything Mack and I would do anything for, it was family.

I sucked in a breath, an idea hitting me.

The universe couldn't have Dath... but maybe there was a way we could shrink it a little for him. I couldn't warp space or time, but I could do heaps of other things.

"Sleep it off, baby," I whispered, stroking the window as though it were his cheek. "We'll be here when you're ready, and so will everyone else."

Assuming the universe and I could play nice until then.

CHAPTER TEN
Touching Danu

Dath
Sunday, February 1st

Blessed be Imbolc… for everyone else, because this situation sucked so hard.

I was awake—that was the good news. I suppose the even better news was that I'd been cleared as non-infectious and allowed to stay in a regular room in the medical bay, rather than being cooped up in the isolation room any longer than necessary.

Of course, the better news came with the bitter: I was *still in* the med bay, not allowed to leave or go back to any semblance of regular life. I'd been in here a week since collapsing in the hall during the lockdown alert, but I still felt miserable, even with all the fluids, meds, and everything they offered to fix what was wrong with me. At least they'd stopped sedating me. I'd been awake for two days now, groggy and ever-increasingly annoyed I was conscious, reminded of what I couldn't do. The medical staff allowed me to get up and wander the bay in small doses, and that helped a little, while also crushing my heart into what felt like a tiny little rubber ball that was being ping-ponged about, ricocheting off every emotion I had.

I glared at the romance novel in my hand, then tossed it at the black chair by the window to my left. The book skidded across the seat, slipped through the open space in the back, and hit the floor. I was a thousand percent done with this, lying here in an uncomfortable bed in nothing but a hospital gown. I had a life, *dammit*. I'd left Alpha Centauri where I'd found it—in one piece, even—so this? *This* was bullshit. My mission was over, and I certainly wasn't interested in the parting gift I'd brought home.

Mostly I was just pissed to still be *here*, on Crosspoint.

I should've been on Earth as of a couple days ago. Right now, it would be late afternoon at home, where my grove would start to gather and catch up with each other and do a craft or two before the ritual. Earlier today, I would've spent time with Mom and Callie, making things for our altars and blessing them, while drinking ice wine and warm cider paired with freshly baked honey oatmeal cookies and apple turnovers to battle the chills of Canadian winter. It would've been a perfect, gentle way to get back to the life I'd had; the one I'd been trying to recapture ever since I'd come back.

The truth was I hadn't managed to recapture

much: I hadn't crossed over the threshold yet, hadn't reclaimed anything of myself, not really. It felt like being in a dozen rough pieces and trying to put them back together from the middle—only that middle rotated and changed pace, kind of like a merry-go-round that allowed for blurred glimpses of where I wanted to be but never quite let me get off. I'd never signed up for that particular ride, and sometimes I had to question why I'd even attended the carnival.

I glanced at the book on the floor, a small smile itching at my lips. Although I hadn't recaptured or reclaimed myself, I'd been offered a taste of renewal that led to something brand new and exciting: a future with Mack and Kytzia, precious moments woven together around a peace of mind that had taken root deep inside and finally found its blossoms. And what blossoms they were: colourful and bright like a fiery rainbow, fluffy and soft like dandelion wishes, and so full of life they could burst.

Dammit. I felt awful for dragging Kytzia and Mack into potential danger because of me. I couldn't even get out of here to apologize properly—to take care of them, post-medical scare.

Thankfully, whatever I had wasn't contagious. They weren't infected, and neither was anyone else. No one else had to suffer—only me. The condition was contained internally, at least for now, or so the doctors figured. Some kind of alien life-form had gotten into my body, apparently, and made itself at home.

The current theory was that I picked it up just before I returned to Crosspoint, but no one had known to look for it and no one had seen it in the tests—mostly because they hadn't realized what they needed to look for, part of the danger of sending teams to planets and solar systems we didn't know. The going theory was that it started out as a tiny little thing—a fleck of dust, really—that crawled in through my ear, grew, then put pressure on my brain. The rest of their theory was that I'd attracted the multi-cellular, not-quite-plant-or-animal-but-we'll-call-it-a-bug-anyway through the plants I'd been working with, and it could've had something to do with a symbiotic relationship I'd disrupted, though they didn't know exactly which ones yet. Those tests were still in the lab. At the moment, rumour said the creature thrived in tissue-dense conditions with a hybrid nature that didn't care what kind of creature its habitat was.

In any event, our visitor had crept under the radar, regardless of the safety procedures I'd taken before and after stepping foot on Crosspoint. It could take weeks for someone in RED to derive the solution that would get this damn thing out of me. There was also the matter of ensuring the thing *remained* contained after that, since there was so little knowledge to work with. And apparently, it didn't appear to want to leave its cushy new abode. According to scans, it'd buried itself in the back of my head instead of hanging out near my sinus cavity or throat, like it'd decided I was a great host and staying was the cool thing to do. Chances were that it would die or leave me if *I* were to die, then either seek out someone new or do something else altogether.

For now, I had to wait and let my colleagues figure it out.

Until then, I could only think of all the catching up on Earth I was missing out on. Not all of it was achievable through vidchat or text message. Some of it needed to be done in person, where we could feed off each other's energy and *feel* connected in a physical way, even if that connection was invisible. Not to mention I still needed to touch ground and feel the pull of the lake. Up here, grounding wasn't the same, no matter how much I tried.

I'd also wanted to show Mack and Kytzia the rest of my life, to let them in all the way. As it was, they'd come to see me these last couple of days, but not as much as I'd hoped. Sure, I'd hate for them to spend all their free time here, but it would've been a relief if they'd hung around. Just the thought of them enjoying downtime together without me left me bummed. Frustrated. Sad. And now I was just plain teary-eyed, tears falling down my cheeks before I realized my gaze had blurred while feeling abandoned and lost to this shit.

Fuck. I was tired and in pain, grossed out and heartbroken, and now I was fucking crying because there wasn't anything else I could do. Why couldn't coming back be easy and happy? Why did my work have to ruin it all? Space exploration was supposed to be entirely too awesome for words… and now I had all the joys of some awful fuckery that was this extraterrestrial asshole that loved my brain and absolutely despised the lockdown alarms, which was why I'd collapsed in the hall to begin with.

Triple Goddess, grant me some fresh perspective, because I was damned tired of looking through my own eyes.

⸻ •••• ⸻

An hour later, a knock rattled my door, followed by Mack and Kytzia stepping into my room, all smiles and cheer, wearing parkas, head coverings, and fingerless gloves.

What in the Norse Hel? I knew I'd had pretty strange dreams while I was knocked out, but this… *Error, error. Does not compute.*

Granted, the black, white, and eggplant-purple toque Kytzia wore was the cutest little nerdy hat, with what I'd readily admit were the most adorable raccoon ears, whiskers, and pompoms, but what was she doing with it *here*?

Was this a dress-up party I'd missed or had someone killed the temperature controls outside of med bay?

"Hey there, babe!" Kytzia hurried to my bedside to plant a damp, glossy kiss on my cheek. "Sorry we're late. How are you feeling today?"

I glanced over Mack's parka—dark blue with black trim, where Kytzia's was white with neon-pink trim—then up to the sparkly black scarf wrapped once around Mack's head, loose enough to not mess with xir hair or the jeweled, green-black feathers and multiple gold hoops of xir earrings. "Um… okay, sort of. Where's the party?"

Mack smiled, sly with a hint of *wouldn't you like to know?* "If you get up, maybe we'll take you there."

"Uhhh…" I peered at the open door behind Mack, seeing a nurse pass by in plum-coloured scrubs. Right. I'd been allowed to wander the rooms around here, but I hadn't been allowed outside of the department. Somehow, I didn't think the doctors would look too kindly on me breaching that set of boundaries…

"It's okay," Kytzia said, brushing her fingers through my hair before looking at Mack. "You've been cleared for today. Doctor Cheche said we could take you on a joyride for a bit. We just have to take it easy," she added, her gaze as serious as her solemn tone. "If you're up for it, that is?"

Hold up. Stay here and wallow in a pity-party for one *or* take a free pass on these cream-coloured walls and enjoy living with them?

"Fuck, yes," I breathed, kissing Kytzia's cheek, relieved she didn't turn away. I was still working up to kissing her and Mack on the lips.

"*Yessss.* Excellent." Kytzia grinned at Mack over her shoulder. Mack was out the door the next second, then returned with a black suitcase.

That wasn't the only thing Mack carried, however: draped over xir other arm was a green patchwork cloak and a staff was in xir hand, looking to be little more than a long piece of steel with symbols etched into it. Symbols I recognized as xe drew close enough for me to see them better: triskeles, mostly, with Celtic knots winding downwards and around, accompanied by a few characters of what looked like the Ogham alphabet.

Blessed Brigit of the Fire, *what was this?*

"What did you do?" My voice wavered as I asked, unable to look Mack in the eye as xe set the suitcase at the end of the bed. I slipped out from under the covers and touched the cloak, a mixture of different shades of green fleece and what could've been cotton. It wasn't mine, but the length and hood reminded me of one I'd owned some time back as a teen, when I'd first made a cloak with Callie. This one was just as rough in terms of skill, but I suspected its purpose was worth its weight in diamonds. It was terrifying and enthralling all at the same time.

"You'll see," Mack sang, unzipping the suitcase. As Kytzia closed the door, Mack took out my things, including a pair of blue jeans, a long-sleeved shirt with green and white stripes, my comfy black and blue sneakers, and a white t-shirt. Wrapped inside the t-shirt, however, were my Awen, triskele, and Tree of Life pendant, along with all of my rings, which had been strung on a piece of green thread to keep them together.

Tearing up, I clutched the Awen and kissed Mack's cheek. The med staff had taken all of my things the day they admitted me, and I'd missed having my talismans anywhere near me. Normally I would've put them all on and lit the candles on my altar, then meditated and called out to the Goddess Brigit to bestow blessings on my loved ones today. Without any of my things near me, I'd felt alone and disoriented, without a hearth or foundation to call my own, unable to feel the connection from within these sterile walls.

"Thank you," I whispered, hugging Mack as I buried my face in xir neck, further comforted by the scent of apples and spice.

"Always welcome." Mack gave me a squeeze and pushed me back. "Now, get dressed or we're going to be late."

•••

With Mack to my left and Kytzia to my right, I was allowed to leave the bay without incident, even receiving smiles from the nurses as I passed.

Part of me felt like I was getting away with something, as if somehow walking out in plain sight counted as sneaking around. There was an air of rebellion to it; a middle finger to life. Inspiration surged through me on a rush of thrill, and I walked the halls to the lift with my head high, never once letting a single stumble deter me.

"You're moving better," Kytzia said as we took the lift to deck twenty-one. She slipped her arm through mine and smiled so prettily I couldn't help but kiss her cheek in thanks for simply being her. "We've been worried, did I mention that?"

"Once or twice." Times a hundred, actually, but I wasn't going to say that. "I'm working on it, though. Promise."

"Good," Mack said, clutching my other hand as we walked through the corridor, "because you can't get rid of us that easily, *a chuisle mo chroí*."

I stopped, taken by the soft words. "Wait, what's that mean?"

"'Pulse of my heart,'" Mack murmured in my

163

ear, xir lips grazing skin. "Gaelic."

I shivered, realization taking hold as the sentiment pawed itself a nice little hole in my heart and curled up inside of it for the keeping.

"Come on," Kytzia said, and pulled me along. When we stopped, we stood outside one of the free-tech rooms. She swiped the touchpad beside the door, once, twice, then again before pressing her palm to it. The door slid open, the scent of cedar and pine hitting me like a strong perfume.

Kytzia didn't let me linger: she tugged down her toque, gave me a playful grin, and led me into the room.

I stopped breathing, stopped moving, stopped thinking. Just a complete stop, though my heart said *screw it* and raced merrily along, thumping away as the door closed behind us. The scene fell into darkness accompanied by a slight, dry chill, as if a mild winter night descended. Stars shone above with a glimpse of the moon.

A copse of trees stood two feet away, lightly dusted with snowflakes like the other trees forming a small wooded area around us that dipped down into a ravine. A series of staggered garden boxes were to my left, covered in a blanket of snow at least half a foot deep. To my right, there was an oak shed and a well-stocked pile of logs.

I recognized those trees, that shed, and when

I looked ahead across the expanse of yard, I knew that grey brick house with its two-floor-plus-basement open plan and solar panels. This was Gina's property; her backyard, specifically, in which our grove met often during the year. It was the yard where they were meeting tonight.

Yet there they were, between us and the house: my grove mates, gathered around a bonfire that looked warmer and more inviting than any sun I'd seen. A dozen of them laughed and mingled as we usually did before a ritual, many of them strangers to me. Half a dozen more moved in and out of the house, some of them carrying items to the ritual space and joining the merriment.

I choked on my breath, puffs of it escaping me into the cold. My grove mates weren't the only ones there, I realized: Callie and Mom stood around the fire, warming their hands, both of them in heavy black cloaks, and Callie's dark hair twisted and tied with white, green, and gold ribbons. Dad joined them the next second, tromping through the snow in big winter boots and a thick, brown cloak with a wolf-coloured faux fur capelet, his shoulder-length brown hair tied back.

Mom and Callie, who should've been elsewhere with their coven. *Dad,* who never came to these celebrations at all. I heard them as clear as day, their voices, their laughter. I saw the looks on their faces, as though they were so excited they could barely contain themselves.

And I stood there crying, unable to do anything else but let tears warm my cheeks.

"I need to—" No other words came, just a soulful ache. Hastily slipping around Mack, I hid behind a tree and wiped my face, though my sniffles attested to the fact that no matter how many times I tried, the tears were there to stay.

A faint, inconsistent crunch of snow followed, as if it were confused between existing and not.

"Hey," Kytzia said softly. Her arms wrapped around my stomach from one side, while Mack hugged me from the other. "It's okay. You can have a bloody good cry. This is for you, anyway. We're following your lead here. They're waiting on you, too."

"What?" I blinked at her. "What is this?" Could it even *be* real? Maybe it was the asshole in my head, but I was so damn confused.

Mack pulled back and brushed my cheeks with xir thumbs, xir smile glowing with the moonlight. "This is you *not* missing your holiday, *mo chroí*. Since you can't go to Earth, Earth's come to you, and we've split the difference. Everyone there? They're the real deal and in real-time."

"But—but—" I sputtered.

"But nothing," Kytzia finished, staring up at me. "The tech was already available, being used for other things. We just needed to set it up in this framework, so we got help from people we know—a few friends who loved the challenge." She shrugged. "We talked to your family, too, to find out what else we could do to make it legit. Gina was all too happy to help, especially with the little bits, like how to make the cloak and staff."

I barely understood a word of what she'd said. My head was still stuck on the impossibility of what was going on.

I guess it showed, because Kytzia laughed and kissed my cheek. "Baby, don't short-circuit yourself. It's a hybrid system we rigged up, between virtual reality and projected video. Half the hardware is here, receiving and projecting, and the other half is down there, doing the same thing, with a bunch of tech in the middle doing all the complicated stuff." She gave me another one of her *I'm bloody brilliant* grins. "You can see them and they can see you, though you're all holograms. You can't *touch* them, but you can see, hear, and hang out with everyone."

Gods... I loved her. She had a mind worth worshipping, and I'd be the first to offer my faith.

Even so, "Why?" was the only thing I could manage to say, my voice cracking.

"Because we care about you," Mack answered, drawing me close. "We're serious about this, about *us*. We want us to be a permanent thing, and it'll take work, but that's good. We'll always work hard to keep this good stuff, 'cause the shitty stuff always comes *way* too easily." Xe eased me back. "You were there for us when things hurt. This is that coming back to you."

"Three-fold," I muttered, glancing through the tree to catch a glimpse of fire.

"Yeah, exactly," Kytzia said and tugged on my hand, "so let's go, babe. Introduce us properly."

Once I found both my feet and my courage, introduce them was exactly what I did. As we marched up to the group, we were greeted with hoots and hollers and huzzahs, air-hugs taking the place of real ones. They looked so real, so *there*, I caught myself forgetting I was still on Crosspoint, still sick, but still so completely in love with Mack and Kytzia that none of the falsehoods mattered. Because as Dad reminded me after I asked him why he'd come when it wasn't his thing: family was at our core, whether it be by blood, choice, or common bond, and *being* family meant doing whatever we could to take care of those we loved.

Without a doubt, Mack and Kytzia earned their Bellin family badges that night. As everyone gathered in a circle around the bonfire to begin the Imbolc ritual, Mack slipped a flat box of Earth dirt from the biology department across the ground in front of me. Blushing, I took my place upon it as Gina led us through the rit, first through a group meditation, then through the purification of our space with water and incense—the scent of which I could smell, but not the stick that went around on Earth. No, the cedar scent came from the incense that Kytzia had lit and kept beside her with a bowl of water, along with a mesh pouch of seeds and nuts that I could make in offering at the same time the others did.

Everything. They'd brought *everything* I'd need, right down to the containers of food they'd snatched from the cafeteria so we could participate in the potluck feast with the others after the rit—so I didn't feel left out or alone.

I couldn't have been more blessed, a fact I noted when I finally kneeled on the box of earth and touched down during our prayer to the Earth Mother, finding that bit of grounding that I'd needed for years. This moment: *this* was what I'd needed, even if it didn't happen quite as I'd expected.

Still, I'd take it, and I'd treasure it, just as I cherished the way Kytzia held my hand during the ritual, giving me the sensation of touch. Just as I adored the time Mack had taken to make a staff from scratch, and the efforts Kytzia had taken to find someone to pull together a simple cloak. They were little things, but they had an impact I couldn't put to words, only feelings. It was the comfort of hearth and home, of family and joyful celebration, of life and blessings and everything that kept us waking up to every new day.

Mack and Kytzia… I loved these quiet, simple, most human moments when I could really see them—feel them—for who they were, right down to their deepest selves. I felt their care and compassion; their love and the warm fuzzies they struck up in me, little fires that kept me going from the heart out. If we were all made of star stuff, then Mack and Kytzia came from the best of the batch. They were my binary star, shiny and beautiful.

More than that, they felt like home. I hadn't known what to expect coming back, but I'd thank every moment I had that they'd chosen me, despite every poor decision and well-meant intention. If this was the tone of our future, I was ready for it. I could spend all my years to come taking care of them and loving them just like this.

Even the darkest, deadliest winter could give way to the brightest, most abundant spring, and I was *there*. My winter was on its way out, as slow as it was in letting me go completely, though my spring had already arrived, as warm and real as the hands around mine.

I'd run off into the darkness but came home to the light. There was no greater hope than that.

EPILOGUE
Ribbons Entwined

Dath
Saturday, May 2nd

Huzzah that I was still alive, because now I could show Kytzia and Mack all the things we could do with ribbons. You know, after we unwound them from the maypole.

The ribbons, that was, not Mack and Kytzia. Though tying the two of *them* to the maypole had occurred to me the entire time my grove mates danced around the pole and taught Mack and Kytzia how to weave in and out with the ribbons. Would've certainly fit the spirit of Beltane.

I snorted. Seated at the picnic table with our drums, I was the self-appointed protector of our lunch as the majority of our group giddily admired the dancers' handiwork in the middle of Gina's backyard where we'd just finished our Beltane ritual. The weave of bright pink, snow-white, mint-green, and buttercup-yellow ribbons was nice and tight around the steel maypole, the crown of flowers on top tilted towards the midafternoon sun. It was a lovely sight, one I was all too happy to witness, my feet firmly on Earth.

Yeah, I was finally Earth-side, and I was taking my four months plus of vacation seriously. Mack and Kytzia had come along to make sure I didn't short-change myself. I knew they also wanted to make sure I was okay, and I welcomed their concern. It gave all of us a chance to spend time with our families, especially the twins, because just talking about them graduating next month made Mack beam with pride.

Kind of like the pride Mack had shown when xe'd given Kytzia and I the Irish Claddagh rings we wore now, our silver rings matching the one Mack wore. The rings were a happy surprise from a couple weeks ago, after I'd been allowed out of the med bay for good.

"Tradition," Mack had said shyly, then slipped the rings on the ring fingers of our right hands with the point of the heart facing our wrists to show we were in a relationship. A crowned heart inside a pair of hands, meant to represent loyalty, friendship, and love? I wasn't about to turn down what Mack wanted to say with that. I'd kissed xem and then some in return, while Kytzia had jacked everything up to a hundred on the sexy scale.

Seriously, tying them to the maypole was sounding better and better.

As for the little shit that had hopped a ride in

my head? It was gone, thankfully. The medical and research teams had found a way to extract the bastard through sound, injections of some concoction they'd come up with, and a touch of surgery, though I was still under observation and scheduled to visit the ground station every week for a check-up. If they'd come up with a proper name for it yet, I didn't care. I wanted to stay well away from the thing, some kind of studded millipede that looked like it'd vomited up a sea anemone and tumbled downhill with a barrel of glue, ending up in a warped, flexy version of a porcupine. Maybe one day I'd ask for the whole story—maybe I'd even want to talk about it and come to terms with the ordeal—but it was too soon. I could leave the station, that's all that I cared about right now. I was just thankful I was still on this side of the Veil, because while that barrier was thin at Beltane like it was at Samhain, I certainly wasn't ready to cross over to be with the dead. I still had things to do.

Like wrap Kytzia up in pink ribbon and watch Mack tickle her feet into oblivion.

Yeah, traditions… I think we needed to make a few new ones, because while three was a magical number, it was also half of a heart-shaped symbol that could be made whole with the right point—one I'd found waiting in the cosmos, ready to shine, melding three hearts into one. It was a true wonder of the heavens, wrapped in the glittering beauty of stardust, and one I'd never leave behind again.

Our past was our past, shared and forgiven. There was only one direction for us now: forward, come whatever may. Everything else was simply part of a journey worth taking.

Fin

GLOSSARY

Aengus (Angus Mac Óg) — Celtic God of youth, love, and beauty. Son of the Dagda and the river goddess, Boann. Husband of Caer Ibormeith, for whom He changed himself into a great white swan after correctly identifying Her among 150 other swans.

Awen — Both a universal force and the neo-Druid symbol—/|\—which consists of three vertical lines, where the outer two lines lean towards the middle line and converge at the top but do not touch. Sometimes they are accompanied by three circles at the top. The word *Awen* is Gaelic, meaning "inspiration" or "essence," and speaks to multiple forms of inspirations and wisdom, including poetic and divine inspiration, the essence of life and the universal power behind it, the flow of spirit, and spiritual illumination. The Awen symbol may be interpreted as a balance among forces or as any number of triad concepts.

Bast (Bastet) — Egyptian Goddess of cats and protection, depicted with the head of a lion, sand cat, or domestic cat. A daughter of Ra, Bast was a goddess of Lower Egypt who also is part of the group of gods that form the Eye of Ra. She is a warrior, protector of Ra and the Pharaoh, though She is also associated with nurturing aspects and is often depicted holding kittens.

Beltane — [*bel*-tayne or *bel*-tinuh] — A Celtic Fire Festival and holiday that occurs between the spring equinox and summer solstice. It is the start of the light half of the year and celebrates life, love, and the renewal of the earth. It is celebrated with dancing and merriment, though it is also associated with passion, fertility, and desire. In present day, Beltane is celebrated on May 1 in the Northern hemisphere (also known as May Day) and October 31 in the Southern hemisphere.

Blót — [bloat] — A common Heathen rite, done to achieve a specific purpose such as honouring a particular god or goddess, celebrating a holiday or special occasion such as a birth or marriage, or even as a devotional rite. It is a time to make offerings of gifts, food, drink, hospitality, and gratitude to the gods and goddesses in exchange for Their blessings and help. It is also a means to strengthen the community and kindred by bringing folk together.

Brigit — Celtic Goddess of poetry, healing, midwifery, and smithcraft. She is a triple goddess and one of the most honoured deities of the Celtic pantheon. Fire is associated strongly with Her, as Brigit symbolizes the fire of the forge, healing, and poetic inspiration. She is daughter of the Dagda and the river goddess, Boann. Imbolc is the holiday most associated with Brigit.

Caer Ibormeith — [*ky-er iv*-ar-vayth] — Celtic Goddess of dreams, prophecy, and sleep. She is a shapeshifter goddess, said to undergo a transformation each year at Samhain, changing between human and swan. Caer chose her mate, Aengus, by appearing to Him in His dreams.

The Cailleach — [*kal*-yahk] — "The Veiled One", an ancient Goddess of the Celts who rules the dark half of the year from winter to summer. A creation goddess, said to have once ruled all the world with cold and winter, during which the green things slept beneath her icy cloak until She was brought to sorrow and her heart melted, thawing the cold. Depicted as an old woman and divine hag with one eye, associated with weather, wisdom, seasonal rites, and wilderness. She is a goddess of life and death, credited with making many mountains and large hills, as well as protecting wild animals, especially deer and wolves.

Cernunnos — [*ker*-noo-nohs] — "The Horned One", a Celtic God of animals, trees, Nature, and wilderness. He appears in human form with antlers or horns and is a god of natural forces, associated with fertility, prosperity, the earth, love, hunting, and death.

Cerridwen — [ker-*id*-wen] — Celtic Goddess of wisdom, old age, rebirth, transformation, and keeper of the sacred cauldron of knowledge, inspiration, and rebirth. She is a patroness of bards and has great magic, including the ability to shapeshift.

The Dagda — [*dagh*-the or *dagh*-dha] — The Celtic God known as the "King of the Gods" and "Father of Tribes", where *Dagda* ("The Good God") refers to His ability to excel at many skills. He is considered a sun god, associated with abundance and knowledge, presented as a wise old man with one eye and husband to the Goddess Boann. He possesses a great cauldron of bounty and rebirth that can feed armies, a club that can kill nine men in a single blow with one end and revive the dead with the other, and a harp that obeys his commands and can put an entire assembly to sleep or make them laugh and cry.

Danu (Anu) — A Celtic creation Goddess and mother of their gods. She is a fertility goddess for whom the Tuatha de Dannan are named and is associated with the earth, rivers, wells, water, prophecy, magic, and wisdom, representing the power of the land and sovereignty. She is also considered an aspect of the triple goddess, the Mórrígan, and an early form of Anu, the universal mother.

Druid — A practitioner of Druidry, a neo-pagan spirituality that draws inspiration from the beliefs, traditions, and gods of the ancient Celtic peoples. In ancient times, Druids were a professional class with great influence among their people, not only as religious leaders, but as teachers, philosophers, advisors, adjudicators, and healers. Modern-day Druidry is a nature-based practice without a set belief system, though at its core are the sacredness of nature, knowledge, interconnectedness, and the ancestors.

Freyja (Freya) — Norse Goddess of love, health, magic, battle, desire, sex, prosperity, abundance, wealth, and power. She is one of the Vanir's mightiest gods and twin to the God Freyr. When warriors are slain in battle, Freyja is first to take half of the fallen to Her hall, while Odin's Valkyries take the other half to Valhalla. She is also a guardian of the Vanir gods and leader of the Disir, female ancestors who protect their families and act as intermediaries for people and the gods.

Frigga (Frige) — The Norse All-Mother and Æsir Goddess of wisdom, marriage, childbirth, female strength and power, and right order. She is the Lady of Asgard, wife to Odin, and is said to be a great seer who knows all fates but says nothing of them. Frigga maintains order, including domestic order, and is a patroness of spinning and weaving. There are twelve goddesses known as her handmaidens (trusted companions), though they may also be forms Frigga takes to interact in the world. "Friday" is derived from Her name.

Heathen — A practitioner of Heathenry (also known as Germanic Neopaganism and Ásatrú/Asatru), as well as a descriptor applied to aspects of Heathenry, the modern revival of the beliefs and traditions of the ancient Germanic peoples of northern Europe, including the Norse and Anglo-Saxons. They are polytheists who worship multiple gods, such as Odin, Thor, and Freyja, as well as nature spirits, ancestors, and the Norns. Present-day Heathens model their traditions and values after the practices found in the ancient Germanic lore, history, cosmology, cultures, and archeological evidence.

Hekate (Ἑκάτη, Hecate) — [e-KAH-tee or eck-AA-tee] — Greek Goddess of crossroads, the night, magic, entrance ways, light, knowledge of herbs and poisonous plants, witchcraft, ghosts, and necromancy. She is a protective triple goddess who can bestow prosperity, victory, wisdom, luck, and blessings so long as the receiver deserves them. She is well-known for helping the Goddess Demeter search for Her daughter Persephone, who was taken by Hades. Afterwards, Hekate became Persephone's advisor and companion in Hades and is often depicted holding twin torches. Her parents are said to be Perses and Asteria, both Titans.

Hel (Helheim) — The Norse realm of the dead and Germanic underworld, found at the furthest depths of the roots of the World Tree, Yggdrasil. This is where those who die of natural causes, sickness, and old age reside, as well as those who do not end up somewhere else (such as with their patron god/goddess or with Freyja or Odin if they are a warrior). It is a cheery, peaceful realm, where the Goddess Hella (Hel) offers a home and rest. Most of the ancestors reside there, along with the God Baldr, Odin and Frigga's son.

Imbolc — [*imm*-olk or *im*-bolk] — A Celtic festival and holiday that occurs at the midpoint between winter solstice and spring equinox. Associated with the Goddess Brigit, Imbolc marks the return of light as the dark winter days fade away. Traditionally, it was a "floating holiday" that took place at the start of lambing season, when the first sign of milk was observed in the ewes. It is now celebrated on February 1 (or 2) in the Northern hemisphere and August 1 in the Southern hemisphere.

Loki — A Norse trickster god and Odin's blood brother. Although considered a troublemaker, Loki brought about benefits when making amends, such as getting dwarves to make Odin's spear and Thor's hammer. He also gave birth to Sleipnir after turning into a mare to distract the stallion of a giant who wanted to take Freyja, the sun, and the moon as his fee for building the walls of Asgard. His other children are the Goddess Hella (Hel), Jörmungandr the Midgard Serpent, and Fenrir the wolf. He is bound in Hel beneath a serpent that drips venom, though his wife, Sigyn, catches as much of the venom as She can in a bowl.

The Mórrígan — [*mor*-ree-ghan] — A Celtic Goddess of the earth and sovereignty, as well as sex, fertility, and war, particularly as She favours warriors. Also known as "Great Queen" and "Phantom Queen," She is a triple goddess with many shapes and faces, to whom mortal kings are ritually married. Ravens, crows, and horses are associated with Her.

Odin (Woden) — The Norse All-Father and God of wisdom, divinity, magic, poetry, transformation, war, frenzy, the dead, and runemasters. He is leader of the Æsir gods and lives in Valhalla, though He constantly wanders the worlds and will meddle in people's lives, gaining Him the descriptions of "trickster" and "master of disguise". He is known for His knowledge seeking, going so far as to sacrifice parts of Himself to obtain wisdom, including hanging from the World Tree and trading one of his eyes. He rides an eight-legged steed named Sleipnir, who was birthed by Loki. "Wednesday" is derived from His name.

Ogham — [*ogh*-am or *oh*-am] — An ancient Celtic alphabet, mainly written on stones and wood for use as markers of property, tombstones, and secret messages. The letters are written on a vertical line that links them together, and messages are read from bottom to top. The original twenty letters are a collection of horizontal and diagonal lines that either touch or cross the central line. Those letters are grouped into four *aicme* of five letters each: the first set is drawn to the right of the line, the next set to the left, followed by a set of diagonal lines across, then a final set of straight across. Five more letters were added at a later time, though they are not linear symbols. The Ogham is also used for divination, similar to Norse runes, including in the Tree Ogham, where each letter is paired with a tree or plant.

Pentacle — A five-pointed star (pentagram) contained within a circle, usually upright, with the lines that create the star crossing through the centre and each other. The symbol is commonly worn and used by Wiccans and other Pagans. Considered a symbol of protection, the pentacle most often represents the five magical elements of creation: earth, air, fire, water, and spirit, which is the top point. The circle represents unity, infinity, wholeness, and the circle of life, which binds the elements together and brings them into harmony.

Seidr (Seidh) — [saythe] — A type of Norse magic that is shamanic in nature. Freyja is best known for seidr magic, while Odin is the only male god known to practice it, possibly having learned it from Freyja. Practitioners use trance states to roam the other realms in a spirit journey. Seidr is also used in an oracular manner, though it could be worked to do other things, such as contact the dead, communicate with other spirits, or provide protection.

Sumble (Symbel) — A sacred Heathen rite to toast the gods, praise ancestors, strengthen kinship, make oaths, tell stories, and commit oneself to personal growth. The ritual involves drinking from a drinking horn (often alcohol, though not necessarily) that is passed around from individual to individual. The first round is dedicated to the gods, the second round is to remember the dead and heroes, and the third round (plus any further rounds) are for whatever the participants wish to say, whether it be a boast, an oath, or personal goals.

Thor — A Norse God of protection, well-being, and weather (especially thunder), though He is also well-known for his care, compassion, and comfort. He is an Æsir god, son of Odin and Jorah (Earth), a giantess, and husband to the Goddess Sif. As a warrior god, He has a hammer named Mjolnir, which represents power, fertility, protection, and is a symbol of the Heathen tradition. He is the only one of their gods that can cross between worlds on his own, without using some sort of item or help, and His journeys often included Loki. "Thursday" is derived from His name.

Triple moon — A symbol consisting of the three phases of the moon: the crescent of the waxing moon on the left, the circle of the full moon in the centre, and the crescent of the waning moon on the right. It is commonly used by Wiccans and Pagans as a goddess symbol in addition to the lunar cycle, as well as the cycle of birth, life, death, and rebirth.

Triskele — A symbol with three spiral lobes that connect together at a central point, also called a triple spiral or triskelion. It has been used by many cultures, including in ancient Greece and in Celtic history on Irish Mesolithic and Neolithic monuments. The meaning and use of this symbol is diverse and complex. A few particular meanings include: the three realms of Land, Sea, and Sky; past, present, and future; and the interconnectedness of all things.

Wicca — A nature-based, neo-pagan religion and spirituality, with practices drawn from the beliefs of ancient peoples and new inspirations since its development in the 20th century. There are different traditions and variations, though common beliefs shared among them include morality, magic, and the five primal elements. Often practitioners are duotheistic, worshipping a Goddess and a God, though others may be polytheistic, pantheistic, or monotheistic. Some Wiccans may also identify as witches, while others do not.

PLAYLIST FOR *OF KINDRED AND STARDUST*

(Artists and songs are listed in alphabetical order)

Active Child – Evening Ceremony

Banks – Alibi
Banks – Before I Ever Met You
Banks – You Should Know Where I'm Coming From

Digital Farm Animals – Tokyo Nights (feat. Shaun Frank & Dragonette)
Dotan – Home II

Ed Sheeran – Afire Love
Ed Sheeran – Autumn Leaves
Ed Sheeran – Give Me Love / The Parting Glass
Eisbrecher – Die Hölle muss warten
Ellie Goulding – Only You
Ellie Goulding – Winner
Erik Hassle – No Words
EUZEN – Judged By

Faun – Golden Apples

Gregorian – All I Need
Gregorian – Dark Angel

Hoobastank – A Thousand Words
Hoobastank – Can You Save Me

Imaginary Future – As Long as I Have You, I'm
Home
Imaginary Future – Everything We Need
Imagine Dragons – Dream
Inkubus Sukkubus – Love Spell

Lord of the Dance Soundtrack – Suil a Ruin
Loreena McKennitt – Snow

Nadia Ali – Fantasy

Of Monsters and Men – Black Water
Of Monsters and Men – Human
Of Monsters and Men – Slow Life
Of Monsters and Men – Yellow Light
Of Monsters and Men – Your Bones
Omnia – Fairy Tale
OMNIMAR – Ego Love
OMNIMAR – Out of My Life

Sarah Brightman – Eden (Enigma Remix)
Sarah Polley – Courage
Secret Garden – Prayer
Stone Sour – Hesitate
Susan Craig – Shadow

The xx – Angels
The xx – Fiction
The xx – I Dare You
The xx – Reunion
The xx – Stars

Unheilig – Geboren um zu leben

AUTHOR'S NOTE

Hi there and thank you so much for reading this book! Without readers like you, stories like this would go nowhere. You're the whole reason to keep doing that wording thing. <3

Of Kindred and Stardust was originally written for, and published as, part of a holiday collection call with Less Than Three Press. They were seeking novellas about holidays outside of the mainstream, which gave me the perfect chance to *finally* write something for one of the Druid holidays, which overlaps with those celebrated by Wiccans, eclectic Pagans, and others. I had 8 days to choose from, each of them special in their own way, and ultimately settled on Imbolc because it's the only holiday that was speaking to me enough to get a story out, especially once it decided it needed to be sci-fi!

And here we are, a poly romance that's on the sweeter side, which isn't my usual fare but I wanted to do a lighter story for the season. I don't see many stories (if any) that have real-life neopagan Druidry in them, especially romances, so I wrote one. And I'm both humbled and incredibly grateful that my former publisher gave this story a chance, stepping up and encouraging people like me to share these stories and characters when others would just turn us away. Thank you, Sam, Megan, and Sasha! And as always, a huge thank you to all readers who give it a read! <3 <3 <3

In a nutshell: this is a love story for Imbolc. The way the relationship moves, the personal journeys of the characters, and the overall plot—it's all inspired by Imbolc, and the significance of the holiday weaves throughout the story since Imbolc is about renewal, rebirth, and more. It's a time of great reflection and pushing forward, caught between Winter Solstice and the Spring Equinox. It's a time of celebration, joy, relief, and hope because the dark half of the year (aka. cold-as-heck winter for many of us!) is heading out and spring is coming, bringing growth and life that's going to blossom into so much more. And so follows Dath's relationship with Mack and Kytzia. It all goes together in the spirit of the festival, right on through to the various aspects of the goddess Brigit!

This story has so much personal significance and experience packed into it. Dath's voice is very… me and being inside his head is like taking a trip into mine. There's also a lot of my partner in this and our experiences with our

Pagan community, which has been so very kind, gracious, and open to us both. This is a shout-out to all of them and the love for life, family, and everything they've shared with us… just set in the future, because I'm curious about what Paganism will look like 80 years from now, especially with all of our tech and how it keeps growing, along with our interest in space exploration. Nature and knowledge are integral to Druidry, so I ran long and far with them. And for anyone who doesn't have any idea what I'm talking about, here are major organizations that can hook you up with info: ADF (Ár nDraíocht Féin), OBOD (Order of Bards, Ovates and Druids), AODA (Ancient Order of Druids in America), and the Druid Network! We're a rather diverse bunch. ^_^

I also wanted to play with one possibility for how the future could look in space, taking into account everything going on right now, particularly with all of the advances being made in astronomy (the super-awesome data from the Kepler space telescope is going to keep folks busy for a while!) and the likes of the various national space agencies, SpaceX, Blue Origin, and Boeing working on ways to take space exploration and tourism to the next level. Add that to so many other factors, including the Millennial generation—how they've been born into a highly digital and electronic-heavy world that's becoming more technologically advanced, plus an incredible amount of access to knowledge and each other's ideas—who knows where we'll be in 2099?? Could we have a large space station out there in our solar system by then? At this point, who really knows, especially since 80 years ago, no one would've known we'd have the internet and smartphones or self-driving cars and AIs in constant development by now. They were the stuff of fiction. The future is open to so many things.

So, yeah, that's a little about the story and how it came about! I hope you've enjoyed reading it. For more about what I'm working on these days, feel free to visit my website or find me on social media! My links are on the very last page.

Thank you to everyone who helped bring this story into being, including Nicole Field (thanks for editing the first edition!), Natasha Snow (thanks for the gorgeous cover!), and Less Than Three Press. And thanks to all of you, readers, for being a part of this journey!

Blessings and peace to you all,
Archer

ALSO BY ARCHER KAY LEAH

THE REPUBLIC SERIES
A Question of Counsel (The Republic, book 1)
Four (The Republic, book 2)
Blood Borne (The Republic, book 3)
Soulbound (The Republic, book 4)

NOVELS
For the Clan

NOVELLAS
Heart, Lace, and Soul
Of Kindred and Stardust

HAVE YOU TRIED *THE REPUBLIC* SERIES?

Welcome to *The Republic*, high fantasy romances for across the LGBTQA+ spectrum, where love, fight, and hope are at the very core, entwined with the lives of romantic partners, friends, and families… and maybe a few lifelong enemies, too. Come step into their world where games linger and foul play is afoot!

● ● ●

Democracy. Family. Loyalty. Honour.
The perfect system.

Freedom. Belonging. Unity.
The perfect illusion.

With the right people and the right price, the Republic of Kattal can be brought to its knees.

Peace and security are never a guarantee when greed and lies threaten the balance. Fear and control know no bounds; and sacred tenets don't keep the monsters away. The right to choose can be a nightmare.

But for every line crossed, someone waits on the other side, ready to push back.

In justice, there is wisdom. In wisdom, there is protection. In it all, there is love. Maybe it means saving a village; maybe it means saving someone you can't live without. Sometimes it's just about doing the right thing and learning to love yourself.

Magic may lurk in the shadows.
Crime may never sleep.
But love doesn't back down.

THE REPUBLIC 3
BLOOD
BORNE
ARCHER KAY LEAH

THE REPUBLIC 4
SOULBOUND
ARCHER KAY LEAH

ABOUT THE AUTHOR

Archer Kay Leah was raised in Canada, growing up in a port town at a time when it was starting to become more diverse, both visibly and vocally. Combined with the variety of interests found in Archer's family and the never-ending need to be creative, this diversity inspired a love for toying with characters and their relationships, exploring new experiences and difficult situations.

Archer most enjoys writing speculative fiction and is engaged in a very particular love affair with fantasy, especially when it is dark and emotionally charged. When not reading and writing for work or play, Archer is a geek with too many hobbies and keeps busy with other creative endeavors, a music addiction, and whatever else comes along. Archer lives in London, Ontario with a non-binary partner who loves video games, composing music, and all things out there in the vast space of the universe.

Website: archerkayleah.wordpress.com
Goodreads: goodreads.com/ArcherKayLeah
Facebook: facebook.com/ArcherKayLeah
Twitter: twitter.com/archerkayleah